THE INVISIBLE DETECTIVE

FACES OF EVIL

BY JUSTIN RICHARDS

SIMON AND SCHUSTER

SIMON AND SCHUSTER

This edition published in Great Britain by Simon & Schuster UK Ltd, 2005
First published in Great Britain by Pocket Books,
an imprint of Simon & Schuster UK Ltd, 2004
A Viacom company

1 3 5 7 9 10 8 6 4 2

Simon & Schuster UK Ltd
Africa House
64-78 Kingsway
London WC2B 6AH

A CIP catalogue record for this book is available from the British Library

ISBN 1416901779

Printed and bound in Great Britain by Cox & Wyman Ltd, Reading, Berkshire

For the children and staff of the
Ferncumbe Primary School at Hatton
– the first fans and kindest critics of
The Invisible Detective

Chapter 1

On a cold Monday evening early in 1937, the Invisible Detective held a consulting session accompanied by a barrel organ.

The grandiose blare was intermittent and came from the road outside. There were rather fewer people in attendance than usual, but those who were there could hear the organ, and a merry-go-round, and the husky shouts of stallholders, and the high-pitched laughter of children.

Brandon Lake – the Invisible Detective himself – had to shout to be heard above the noise outside. The fair had taken over part of Cannon Street and most of the smaller roads around. It had arrived, unannounced, on Friday evening and showed no sign of moving on.

The presence of the fair also accounted for the meagre attendance, Jonny Levin thought. He stood concealed behind the curtain in the dimly lit room above Mr Jerrickson the locksmith's shop. On the other side of the curtain, the Invisible Detective sat all but hidden from his audience – his large armchair turned away from them so that his face could not be seen.

For once Jonny was not watching the Invisible Detective, not listening to every wise word and stealing glimpses of anyone asking a question. He was looking out of the window. Why go along to another Invisible Detective session when the fair was in town? Well, given the choice, he would go to the fair. Wouldn't he? Jonny's reflection seemed to wonder the same thing – staring back at him, lean, dark-haired and slightly distorted in the old glass of the windowpane.

But the session had to be held, just like every other Monday since the Invisible Detective had first 'appeared'. Even if few people had bothered to attend and even if you could hardly hear a word that Brandon Lake said.

'Pay attention!' a voice hissed in Jonny's ear, and he jumped, almost bumping his nose on the window.

It was Meg. He could see her mass of auburn hair reflected next to his image in the glass now he looked. 'I was checking to see if Flinch was all right,' he told her.

'Of course you were.'

She knew he was lying. She always knew – whenever *anyone* was lying. There was no point in protesting. Jonny hesitated a moment longer, easing his conscience slightly by checking that Flinch was indeed all right. She was standing beside the coconut shy, a small, slightly bedraggled figure huddled into a coat that was too big, bouncing with excitement and stamping her feet as a wooden ball smashed squarely into one of the coconuts. It didn't move. Probably glued in place, Jonny thought, as he turned away.

He joined Meg at the curtain and peered back into the dimly lit room, struggling to hear what was being said.

'Where's your fishing rod?' Meg whispered.

Jonny nodded back at where he had left the rod, propped against the windowframe. It was the one way they could communicate with the Invisible Detective without being seen – casting small notes across the gap between the curtains and the chair where he sat, turned away from the audience so that only his hand, his hat and the hint of his coat were visible.

That, together with the fact that nobody ever saw him arrive or leave a consulting session, had earned him his title. Jonny, Meg and Flinch knew just how invisible he really was. And Art of course. They were the Cannoniers, and they knew that Brandon Lake did not actually exist.

But the illusion was maintained and the detective's reputation flourished. One of his biggest admirers was speaking now – Albert Norris, the landlord of the local pub, the Dog and Goose. Jonny strained to hear what the man was saying.

'The thing is, she's usually so reliable.'

'Who's he talking about?' Jonny murmured to Meg.

'Elsie, his barmaid.' She turned to glare at him for a moment. 'If you paid attention, you wouldn't have to ask.'

Jonny did not reply, but struggled instead to hear what Norris was now saying, his voice battling with the organ outside.

'No note, no message. Nothing.'

'You say she went to the fair?' The detective had to repeat this twice before Norris heard him properly.

'That's right. But that was on Friday evening, when it first arrived. I gave her the time off as we were quiet. People were more interested in the fair that night.' He sounded aggrieved at the loss of business.

'And she didn't come back?'

'Couldn't say for certain,' Norris admitted. 'She has a small room above the pub, on account of she looks after the rooms. You know, we have two rooms we let out. When they're used, Elsie does the cleaning and makes the beds.'

'You expected her back?' Brandon Lake asked, his strained and husky voice suddenly clear in a moment of near-silence from outside between tunes.

'Thought I heard the door, thought it was her coming in,' Norris said. 'But I was out early on Saturday morning. Didn't realise I'd not seen her until I opened up for the evening. And there's Elsie – gone.' Jonny could see the vague outline of Norris as he shook his head. 'She's never gone missing before. Always reliable. I thought maybe she was ill, but her room was empty. And she's not been back.'

There was a pause as the detective considered this. 'Did you notice if her things were still in her room?'

'They're there all right,' Norris assured him. 'I checked on the Sunday. Like I said, she was so reliable, I never thought she might have done a runner. She could have had bad news and been called away. Only her stuff's all there. Clothes, picture of her mum . . . everything.'

'How very extraordinary,' the detective admitted.

Jonny could hear the shrug in Norris's voice. 'So I thought I'd best talk to you.'

'Indeed. And you may rest assured that I shall make enquiries about Elsie and hope to be able to report my findings when we meet again next Monday.'

Norris seemed happy with this. 'If you find her, sir, you will tell her, won't you? I mean, she's not in trouble or anything. But I can't just keep her job open till she comes back, can I?'

Norris's was the only enquiry of the session. Nobody else seemed keen to pitch their voice against the barrel organ and the sounds of the fair. Faced with the constant noise, people were reminded that others were out there enjoying themselves and many of them had drifted away almost from the start. By the time Norris had finished speaking, there was a general movement towards the stairs. People shuffled away, and as the Invisible Detective assured everyone that he would do his best to find Elsie and wished them all well for the week ahead, his voice was drowned out not by the organ outside but by the sound of footsteps on bare floorboards inside.

Jonny and Meg waited until the room had emptied before coming out from behind the curtains.

'Any more of that and I'll have no voice left,' the figure in the chair said rather huskily as he hauled himself to his feet and shrugged off the enormous overcoat that smothered him. Art Drake folded the coat and dumped it on the chair beside the hat he had been wearing. A simple disguise to make a fourteen-year-old boy look like a middle-aged detective, aided by the dim light and the fact that he sat facing away from his audience. The hardest part, Jonny knew, was deepening his voice. Having to shout against the noise from outside had not helped, he was sure.

'Not much in the tin today,' Meg said glumly, checking how many people had paid sixpence to put a question to the Invisible Detective. 'A shilling.'

'Good old Albert Norris,' Art said. 'And Mrs Carruthers owed us for last week, remember?'

'Flinch will be disappointed,' Jonny said. 'She was hoping we'd get enough to have a go on the merry-go-round.'

'I thought she wanted candyfloss,' Meg said.

Art laughed. 'And she told me she was desperate to see inside the mirror maze. You know – set up in the old gallery on Pembroke Street.'

Meg sighed. 'She just wants to do everything.'

'Of course she does,' Art said gently. 'And,' he added, 'so do I. Come on, I've not really had a chance to look round the fair yet. Let's at least see what's there, even if we can't afford a go on everything.'

'Race you down the stairs,' Jonny offered. But neither Art nor Meg took him seriously – he could give them a head start and still get to where Flinch was waiting outside before they were even halfway there.

'Let's walk,' Art said. 'Save our energy. And besides, we don't want to attract attention. There's always someone waiting to see if they can spot Brandon Lake leaving the session. We don't want them to realise that three kids who didn't seem to be there before have suddenly appeared, do we?'

'No one will spot Brandon Lake,' Jonny murmured as he followed his friends down the stairs. 'He's the *Invisible* Detective.'

One thing Flinch was sure she did not want to do at the fair was to try her luck on the coconut shy. Having watched several people take their turns, she was pretty certain that luck had nothing to do with it.

'It's fixed,' she told Jonny when he arrived.

Meg and Art were pushing their way through a group of people some way behind.

'The *coconuts* are fixed,' Jonny said. 'I was watching from the window.'

'Did we get a case? Anything to investigate?' Flinch demanded. 'I don't like coconuts anyway,' she added, in case there was any doubt.

Art had arrived in time to catch her words. 'Elsie, the barmaid from the Dog and Goose, is missing,' he said.

Flinch wrinkled her nose. 'Probably just run off.'

'Albert Norris is quite worried,' Jonny told her.

'And she's left her stuff behind,' Meg added.

'Stuff?'

Flinch didn't have any 'stuff'. Her home was the disused carpet warehouse where the Cannoniers met and which they used as their den. If she ever had to move, she would have no packing to do.

'Albert Norris said that Elsie was coming to the fair,' Art said. 'So I suggest Flinch shows us round and we can get some idea of what might have happened.'

It sounded like a good plan. But, of course, as soon as they had bought candyfloss, watched the jugglers, listened to the barrel organ and seen the sideshows and stalls, all four of them had forgotten about Elsie.

As the others had expected, Flinch was disappointed they had not got enough money to go on everything, but Art and Jonny said they didn't mind if Meg and Flinch went on the merry-go-round. Meg made a face.

'Why would I want to go on that?' she demanded.

'To keep Flinch company,' Art replied quietly. 'Besides,' he added, winking at Flinch, 'you'll enjoy it.'

'I won't.'

Flinch dragged the older girl to the line of people waiting to hand over their pennies. Meg stood in the queue with her arms folded and saying nothing. When they had paid, Flinch ran to the nearest free horse, Meg taking the one behind. Before long the merry-go-round was turning noisily, and the horses were rising and falling as they spun. Flinch waved to Art and Jonny, her other arm tight round her horse's wooden neck.

Jonny grinned and waved back. Art was pointing behind her, and Flinch risked a quick look back over her shoulder as the horse paused between fall and rise.

She saw Meg, serene in the saddle of the horse behind, her auburn hair blowing out behind her like a mane. Uncharacteristically, she was laughing, her face one huge grin and her eyes wide and alive with enjoyment. She caught sight of Flinch watching her and for a moment she looked guilty and sullen. But then her horse plunged downwards, and the shriek of her laughter reached Flinch above the sound of the wind and the organ and the merry-go-round itself.

* * *

11

Art had enough money left to buy a bag of roasted chestnuts – most of which he knew Flinch would eat. The others would let her, as they were all aware that she had probably not had a decent meal that day. He made a point of not asking Meg if she had enjoyed the ride on the merry-go-round, and nudged Jonny into silence when it looked as if he was going to ask.

'I wanted to do the mirrors,' Flinch said again, rather indistinctly as her mouth was full of chestnuts.

'We've no money left,' Meg told her.

'Another day,' Jonny said. 'It looks like the fair will be here for a while yet.'

Art could see that Flinch was disappointed and he put his arm round her shoulder. 'Why don't we go and have a look – see where it is? Then we can go straight there next time.'

The young girl brightened a little at this and helped herself to another chestnut. 'Yes, let's do that,' she agreed as she peeled the shell off with her grimy thumbnail.

The Amazing Mirror Maze was set up in the Wilkinson Gallery on Pembroke Street. Art had never been inside, but it looked as if one of the rooms had been set aside for the mirrors. There was a tin on a chair by the door and a sign inviting patrons to pay tuppence if there was nobody there to collect the money from them.

'We could just go in,' Flinch said, seeing that the tin was unattended.

'No, we couldn't,' Art told her. 'That would be dishonest.'

'We'd be quick,' Flinch said, but Art could tell she wasn't going to push it, despite her disappointment.

'We'll come back tomorrow,' Meg promised.

'What's that up there?' Jonny asked.

Whether he was really curious or just trying to distract Flinch, Art did not know. But he turned to see where Jonny was pointing.

At the bottom of Pembroke Street was a caravan. It was positioned across the street, as if to mark the end of the fair. There was a group of people in front of it, obviously watching something – a show of some sort perhaps.

'Let's go and have a look,' Art suggested.

As they approached, Art could see that the caravan was actually two caravans positioned close together, at an angle. The one across the street was a typical fairground caravan with steps at the back up to a small door. But alongside it, on the pavement, was another caravan that was more like a circus cage on wheels. A man was standing in front of the cage, addressing a group of people. He seemed taller than everyone else and Art guessed that this was because he was standing on a box or a step.

But it was not the man who held their interest as they joined the group. It was the ape.

'The only one in captivity anywhere in the world,' the man was announcing. 'A cross between a gorilla and an orang-utan. He was found in the jungles of Borneo and used as a ship's stoker for five years before I came across him and set him free.'

'Call that free?' someone close to Art exclaimed.

By leaning forwards on his tiptoes, Art could see that the huge ape standing beside the showman had its legs shackled by heavy chains. The showman ignored the interruption and continued with his patter.

The ape was enormous. It was almost as tall

as the showman – who was indeed standing on a wooden box – and twice as broad. It was covered in light brown hair that was matted and stained. Its dark face was twisted into something between a sneer and a grimace, and small, bright eyes peered out with undeniable intelligence. It seemed to be watching the audience, daring them to disagree with anything its master said.

As the showman turned to address another part of the group, Art was struck by how much like an ape the man himself looked. His jaw jutted forwards and, when he was not gesticulating, his arms hung low by his sides. His dark brown hair was wiry and receding from a heavily lined forehead.

'He's lying,' Meg said quietly to Art.

'Of course. He's here to make money.'

'Set him free and trained him,' the man continued. 'His immense simian intelligence means that he can not only perform simple tricks like some of the other apes but actually understand what I say to him.'

Art could see now that there were more apes in the cage – perhaps four or five of them, crammed into the small space. Two were standing leaning on the bars, as if interested. The others were lying or squatting on the straw-covered floor.

'Show us a trick, then,' a man shouted.

The showman held up his hand. 'All in good time. The Mighty Kong will soon be ready.'

The Mighty Kong nodded in what could have been agreement. One of the other apes rubbed its bottom up at the bars of the cage. Flinch giggled.

'Make it do sums,' another man shouted. 'It did sums last night. Really good, it was.'

The showman had his hand up again, but he seemed to realise it was time for the ape to perform if he was not to lose his audience. 'Very well,' he announced. He turned to the great ape. 'Mighty Kong,' he declaimed, 'tell us please, what is three plus two.' The showman held up his hand close to the ape's head.

Art thought that he was threatening to hit the animal if it got the answer wrong. But in fact quite the opposite happened. The huge ape raised its own paw and clapped it against the showman's hand – once, twice . . . five times in all.

Someone near the front laughed. 'Ah, it just knows to do it five times.'

The showman seemed to have been expecting

16

this. He turned to the man, grinning in a way that was almost threatening. 'Very well, sir, you ask him a question.'

'Keep the answer below twenty,' another man shouted out, 'or we'll be here all night.'

'If you know the answer yourself,' another voice added, to general amusement.

'All right, all right,' the man who had questioned the ape's ability protested. 'Try this, then, Kong. What's nine, take away six?'

Flinch was pushing through the people to get a better view. Art watched her force her way into a narrow gap between a man and a woman without either of them seeming to notice. Meanwhile, the ape was again striking the showman's hand.

The crowd began to count out loud: 'One. Two. Three.'

For a second the ape looked as if it might clap hands again. The showman kept his own hand raised as if to make it clear that he was offering no clues. But the ape's arm dropped to its side and it turned away, satisfied that three was the correct answer.

People moved on from in front of Art and

more people arrived behind him. The showman waved a tin at the crowd and collected coins. Before very long, Art and the others were with Flinch in the front row. Flinch was transfixed. Meg was shuffling her feet, bored. Jonny seemed vaguely interested. Art felt the novelty was wearing off as the large ape responded to various instructions, including, 'Nod your head', 'Stamp your feet' and even – to Flinch's undisguised delight – 'Play dead'. At this, the ape collapsed to the ground, rolled over on its back and stuck its massive front paws in the air.

But even Meg was impressed when the showman produced three tennis balls and tossed them one by one to the ape. It caught them and threw them into the air. Before long, the animal was juggling every bit as well as some of the other street performers. The applause and laughter were deafening.

The showman, who had introduced himself to the gathering crowd as Alan Tamworth, went round with his tin again. It was stuck on the end of a long piece of wood so he could hold it out to the crowd and remain close to his ape. Just as before, it was moved back and forth along the front of the crowd and people dropped coins into it.

But this time, the tin hesitated in front of Art and Flinch. Art ignored it, keeping his expression neutral. Flinch was staring at the ape. The tin paused, rattled. Art continued to ignore it – he had no money left.

Then Tamworth, the showman, took a step towards them. 'You been here a long time,' he said, his voice quiet but laced with menace. 'Yet you ain't paid nothing.'

He rattled the tin again and this time Flinch seemed to notice it. She looked at the tin, then she looked at Tamworth.

'No thank you,' she said.

The man's eyes were burning. 'No thank you? You watch my show for twenty minutes and that's all I get – "No thank you"?'

'We don't have any money,' Art said quickly. Beside him he could see Jonny pulling Meg out of sight into the crowd, slipping away.

'Oh, my heart bleeds for you,' Tamworth said. He made a point of looking devastated. 'Well, maybe I should give you some of my money for being such a good audience, then.'

For a horrible moment, Art thought Flinch might agree to this. But Tamworth did not pause long enough to let her. 'You don't just watch the show, then drift away for nothing, sunshine.' He took a step closer to them. Other people were stepping aside now, so that Flinch and Art were standing alone. 'I have to feed the apes and look after them as well as feed myself, you know. Ain't nothing in this life as comes for free.'

'No. No. Of course not,' Art stammered.

The showman turned away and Art breathed a sigh of relief. But Tamworth was turning to address the enormous ape behind him. 'What do you think, Mighty Kong?' He glanced back at Art and Flinch. 'You think they should just be allowed to watch for free, then scarper? Eh?'

The ape took a step towards Art, snarling with anger. The chains round its feet clanked and dragged as it hauled itself forwards. It reached out its enormous paws and snarled again.

Art was immobile, watching in disbelief as the thing lurched towards him. Then Flinch was grabbing his arm and dragging him away. He turned and they both ran, pushing through the crowd of people, who moved aside for them.

And behind them, following them, came the snarl of the ape and the laughter of the showman.

If Art had stayed for a few more minutes, he would have seen the end of the show. If he had still been there he would have seen Tamworth unlock the cage and gesture for the Mighty Kong to return to his fellow apes. He would have seen the huge creature settle itself down in the cage, the others hurriedly making room, apparently wary of their companion.

And if he had waited a little longer, he might have seen the shadowy, hunched figure watching from the shadows, might have heard it muttering to itself as it lurched uncertainly, painfully, towards the showman's caravan . . .

It was difficult for Arthur Drake to see past the weekend. Somehow it seemed to interfere with all his plans. Despite his dad's assurances that they were only going to be away for a couple of days, it got in the way. They were leaving on Friday, straight from school.

He wanted to use the mysterious clock, the one that he had found in the cellar of a haunted house, to communicate with Art back in the 1930s. Would there be time before the weekend?

He also wanted to see his grandad – the 'original' Art Drake, who had invented the Invisible Detective when he was about the same age as Arthur himself was now. Since finding the casebook of the Invisible Detective and discovering that it was written by someone with the same name as himself, living at the same address and with identical handwriting, Arthur had been drawn more and more into the past. He could speak to Art – sometimes – using the clock. And his grandfather could remember – sometimes – how he had spoken to a boy of his own age and of similar appearance who seemed to be from seventy years in the future . . .

Sarah Bustle, who ran a website version of the Invisible Detective and who knew more about the original than she was letting on, wanted to talk to him. Arthur enjoyed being with her. They had spent half-term on holiday together in Cornwall, though as they had been caught up in a ghostly adventure, there had not been a lot of time to relax and discuss the Invisible Detective.

And just as Arthur had thought he was beginning to understand it all, Dad had won this holiday.

They had won holidays before. Usually someone rang up at just the wrong moment in the evening and invited Arthur's dad along to a two-hour presentation at an inconvenient time where he could book his free holiday and collect some prize or other. There was never any catch . . . or so they said. But Dad never bothered. He didn't get enough time off from his work as a detective at Scotland Yard to take long or exotic holidays. And with Arthur at school, they couldn't go during term time.

But on this occasion there had been no phone call. The invitation arrived in the post – for a long weekend at a country house hotel only fifty miles away. A weekend for two – Peter Drake and his son, Arthur. This weekend.

'It's only for a couple of days,' Dad kept reminding him. But even so, Arthur was not looking forward to it. He liked being at home. He had so much he wanted to do – not to mention homework, which he really *ought* to do.

On Wednesday Arthur managed to get to the haunted house on Jursall Street. It was already growing dark as he made his way past the other boarded-up and deserted buildings on the street to number 7. The door was unlocked, but nobody ever went there because it was haunted. Nobody apart from Arthur and Sarah. She went there to escape from the noise her small brother, Paul, made at home. He went there to go to the cellar.

Once in the cellar, Arthur struggled to hold his torch still while he took the clock from his school bag. It was a simple carriage clock, with the name inscribed on the back scratched off. It seemed not to work, but Arthur wound it up anyway and placed it on the narrow step within a whitewashed alcove.

As he stepped away, he could see that the hands of the clock were already spinning rapidly backwards. 'Come on,' he breathed, glancing at his watch to see what the real time was. Dad would expect him home before long. 'Come on.'

It was like looking into a distorting mirror, the sort you might find at a fairground. The fourteen-

24

year-old boy who shimmered into existence in front of Arthur looked exactly like him. Except he was wearing old-fashioned clothes — grey flannel trousers, a white shirt and dark tie, a jacket and a cap. And he was from 1937.

'Hello, Arthur,' the boy said, in Arthur's voice.

'Hi there, Art,' Arthur replied.

Their meetings were always strange and often a little tense. Like friends meeting again after many years and not really knowing what to say to each other or how to say it.

Often, when they finished their conversations and Art had faded back into the previous century, Arthur found he could barely recall a word they had said to each other. And on other occasions, it was as if Art could simply not hear him. If Arthur mentioned something in Art's future, it was as if he had not spoken. Like the time he had tried to warn Art about the Second World War. It was as if someone had pressed the 'mute' button. There were moments, too, when Arthur watched Art mouthing words but no sound came through.

It was almost an hour later when Arthur left the house. But he had no idea what they had found to talk about for all that time. He could remember

25

laughing and joking. He knew that Art had spoken about a street fair and a missing barmaid. He had mentioned a misshapen figure haunting the streets, unless Arthur had dreamed that bit up . . . He would have to check the Invisible Detective's casebook.

If he remembered. The book seemed to work in the same way. He could read pages and then not know what was in them. It was as if time itself held back certain information until Arthur – or Art – was ready for it. Until the *time* was right.

So the next day, Thursday, after school, when he finally had a chance to talk to Sarah as children spilled noisily across the playground, Arthur had no idea if he had found the hunchback within the pages of the casebook or not.

'I've got to get home,' Sarah said as they walked together to the school gate. 'Mum's out, so I have to look after Paul.'

'I'm off straight from school tomorrow. So I won't see you till next week, then,' Arthur said glumly.

Sarah smiled, shaking her long black hair out of her face. 'You're really looking forward to this weekend away, aren't you?'

'I need it like a hole in the head.'

They paused outside the gate.

'Well,' Arthur said at last. 'I'll see you, then.'

'Yes,' she said. 'See you.' As she started walking briskly away, she glanced at a large black car that was drawing up at the kerb beside them, then she looked round and waved. 'Have a good weekend.'

'Yeah. Right.' Arthur waved back and turned to go. As he did so, he almost bumped into the man who was getting out of the car.

He stepped aside, mumbling an apology. But the man seemed to dodge the same way and they almost collided again. It could have been an accident. Except for the way the man put his hand firmly on Arthur's shoulder.

'Arthur Drake?'

Arthur looked up at the man. He was tall and thin. His dark hair was slicked back with what looked like a large amount of oil and he was wearing sunglasses, although it was a dull and cloudy March day. He had an enormous bushy black beard that framed his mouth and grew up into sideburns, so that only his nose was visible between hair and shades.

'Yes?' Arthur was more surprised than worried.

'You are Arthur Drake?'

'Yes.' He was annoyed now. 'And I'm in a hurry. My dad's waiting for me.' The man made no effort to move, so Arthur added slowly and clearly, 'He's a policeman.'

Now the man did move. But he did not stand aside to let Arthur pass. Instead he looked round quickly, as if to check that nobody was watching, still with his hand on Arthur's shoulder. Then he grabbed Arthur's other shoulder and dragged him firmly, swiftly, towards the car.

Chapter 2

It was the next afternoon, in the Cannoniers' den, that Art explained his plan. They were sitting among the rolls of decaying carpet that still lay on the ground. The walls were rotting and the roof leaked, but nobody else came here and it was somewhere for Flinch to call home.

Jonny had brought some biscuits, which Flinch was devouring as if she had not seen food, let alone eaten any, for at least a week. She was sitting cross-legged on the bare wooden floorboards. Art sat on one of the old rolls of carpet. The dust was so heavy in the air that it was as if they were eating that too. Art could almost taste the dry, decaying wool as he watched the crumbs escaping from Flinch's enthusiastic mouth. Jonny and Meg were perched on another carpet roll opposite. Jonny was grinning and Meg had her arms folded, her expression neutral.

'Why you and Jonny?' Meg demanded.

'Because we'll be the best at it,' Jonny said quickly.

He shuffled along the carpet, away from

Meg, in case she didn't find it funny. But she ignored him.

'Actually,' Art said slowly, 'it's because I think you and Flinch will have more luck than we would at the fair. The stallholders are more likely to talk to you than a couple of boys hanging round. They're more likely to believe that you're friends of Elsie's looking for her. If me or Jonny go asking, they might assume Elsie doesn't want us finding her.'

'Why?' Flinch asked, somewhat indistinctly.

'Old boyfriends,' Meg told her. 'Elsie might be avoiding them.' Her face was still set into its usual dour expression, but Art could tell she was convinced by his argument.

'Which means,' he went on quickly, 'that it's up to Jonny and me to ask in the pub.'

'You hate pubs anyway,' Flinch told Meg.

'That's not the point.'

'But you do.'

'We always allocate the investigations according to who's best suited,' Art said calmly.

'What's that mean?' Flinch wanted to know.

'It means you're going to the fair with Meg tonight,' Jonny told her.

Flinch's face opened into a huge grin. For a moment, Meg almost smiled.

'And it means,' Art added, 'that Jonny and I will need to disguise ourselves.'

'Just so long as you don't try that daft charcoal moustache again,' Meg told Jonny.

'It was very convincing,' he protested.

And that did make Meg smile.

Art had his cap pulled down low over his eyes. He was wearing a coat of his dad's, the sleeves folded back inside themselves so they didn't look too long. He hoped nobody would notice that it reached almost to the floor.

Jonny had indeed resisted the temptation to draw on a moustache with charcoal. But he had rubbed mud on his face to give the appearance of having just come from the gasworks or some other manual job. It looked to Art more like he had fallen in a puddle, but he said nothing. Apart from his face, which was in any case shadowed by his cap, Jonny looked the part. He had on an old, tattered pair of working trousers and a grubby shirt under an old jacket. He made a point of pulling open the jacket every now and again to reveal the bright red braces beneath.

The Dog and Goose was busy. Art hoped it was so crowded that nobody would notice them. He had managed to get two halves of bitter at the bar without looking Albert Norris in the eye. The landlord was so busy with people drifting in from the fair that he hardly spared the boys a glance. They made their way to a couple of seats at a table, taking care to spill beer on the way. By the time they sat down the glasses were only two-thirds full, so they could pretend to drink without actually having to swallow any of the warm, bitter beer. Art risked a sip. It wasn't as bad as he remembered from last time they had disguised themselves to go to the pub, but he still wasn't keen.

There were two men at the table. Before he and Art sat down, Jonny had gestured to the free chairs and grunted something indistinct. One of the men waved to show they were not taken. Now Art tried to think of a way to start a useful conversation. He was aware that Jonny was watching him – his dark eyes glinting from beneath the peak of his cap. Art cleared his throat and one of the men glanced across at him.

'I, er, I thought Elsie would be on tonight,' Art said. Even to himself he sounded slightly nervous. He tried to keep his voice low, but it was still more like a squawk.

The man nodded. He looked at his friend, who nodded back. 'Did you?' the man said. He seemed amused.

'Yes,' Art said, wondering what was so funny.

'Wasting your time,' the second man said.

'Oh?'

'Bit sweet on her, are you?' the second man suggested. He took a swig of beer and wiped his mouth with the back of his hand.

'No, nothing like that,' Art said quickly.

'Bit young to be chasing the ladies too,' the first man said. He had receding dark hair and there was a line of foam trapped in his moustache. 'How old are you anyway?' he wondered, leaning across the table and trying to peer under Art's cap.

'Old enough,' Jonny said.

Both men roared at this.

'Hey, we're only kidding you,' the man with the moustache said when they had calmed down a little. 'Don't take it personal.'

The other man nodded. He was wearing a cap similar to Jonny's, and a fringe of straw-coloured hair was just visible between the brim and his eyes. 'Anyway, our Elsie's gone missing,' he said.

Art and Jonny exchanged looks.

'Really?' Art said. 'What happened?'

The man shrugged. 'No one knows. Just upped and left it seems.'

'Trying to avoid you two maybe,' the man with the moustache suggested. 'Though you're not regulars, are you.' It wasn't meant as a question.

'No,' Jonny admitted. 'But we come in now and again.'

'And you knew Elsie?'

Art nodded and pretended to take a swig of beer. He let some of it dribble down his chin.

'You should talk to Gladys,' the man with the cap said, and before Art could protest, he was on his feet waving across the pub. 'Oi, Gladys,' he shouted loud enough for most people to turn and look. 'Over here – couple of lads want to meet you.'

'Er, no, we don't,' Jonny said. He was looking desperately at Art.

'Not want to meet Gladys?' the man with the moustache said. 'That's a bit rude, isn't it?'

'She's a friend of Elsie's,' the man with the cap explained as a large young woman arrived and dragged up a chair.

Gladys was wearing an awful lot of make-up and a hat that was too small for her head and seemed to perch on top of a mass of improbably blonde hair as if defying gravity. When she grinned, Art could see that one of her front teeth was missing, and when she spoke her voice was deeper than his own.

'What are you on about, Maurice?' she asked the man with the cap. 'I dunno these lads.'

'They were asking after Elsie.'

Gladys pouted in apparent annoyance. 'Well, I can't help 'em. No one can. She's gone.'

'We were wondering if you knew where she had gone,' Art ventured.

'You friends of hers?' From her tone, Gladys did not think this very likely.

'Yes,' Jonny said loudly. 'We are.'

Gladys shrugged. 'Well, I don't know where she is. Just gone.' She sniffed. 'And she didn't say nothing to me about leaving.' It was difficult to tell if Gladys was upset or angry about this.

'Would she have?' Art suggested. 'Would she usually tell you if she was going away?'

'Oh, yes.' Suddenly enthusiastic, Gladys leaned across the table, her hat wobbling precariously. 'She always told me everything. No secrets. Mind you' – she folded her arms – 'that girl couldn't keep a secret if her life depended on it. Always gossiping on about this and that – about what happened here in the pub, who she met, the people in the rooms.' Gladys was nodding emphatically, as if to prove the truth of what she was saying. 'Always rabbit, rabbit, rabbit. Never stopped.'

'Fancy that,' Jonny muttered, glancing at Art.

Art stifled a laugh. 'So, when did you last see her?'

Gladys paused for breath and thought at the same time. 'Must have been Friday lunchtime. I just popped in for a quick . . . visit. She was off to make the beds in the rooms above and sweep them out.' She frowned. 'Why are you so interested anyway? Elsie owe you money or something?'

36

'Nothing like that,' Art said quickly. 'Just concerned.'

'Yeah, well, we're all concerned,' the man with the moustache said. 'Bert Norris is doing his nut, he is.'

The man wearing the cap – Maurice – nodded. 'Even went to see that Invisible Defective bloke.'

'Detective,' Art corrected him.

'You know him?'

Art and Jonny looked at each other.

'Heard of him,' Art admitted.

'Did no good, though. Reckon she's run off with someone.'

The man with the moustache agreed. 'Or the Hunchback of Cricklewood got her,' he added with a laugh.

'The what?' Jonny said, forgetting for the moment to disguise his voice, although no one seemed to notice.

Gladys was more than ready to explain. 'He's a hunchback, they say.'

'In Cricklewood,' Art prompted. It seemed rather unlikely, he thought.

But Gladys was obviously convinced, her

eyes wide as she related the story. 'Might have been Penge. Anyway, he goes round after dark, apparently. And kills people. Does - them - in,' she said, separating each word carefully for maximum effect. 'People only catch glimpses of him. The police are baffled. Been doing it for a year or more, they say.'

'Do they?' Jonny was obviously not convinced either.

But Gladys leaned across the table again, fixing Art with a watery stare. 'And he leaves his victims drained of blood.' She shivered at her own words, making the table rock. 'Ooh,' she went on, shaking her head, 'I need another drink just thinking about it.' She continued to stare pointedly at Art.

Maurice laughed. 'You got him too spooked to get you a drink, Gladys. But it's all right, I'll get 'em in. Same again?'

The fair was just as busy tonight as it had been the previous evening. Flinch seemed happy to wander round, watching people win and lose on the various stalls. She was transfixed by the merry-go-round, but Meg had no money to treat her to another ride. She was saving her few pennies for something else.

'Do you still want to see the mirror maze?' Meg asked as they approached the little art gallery on Pembroke Street.

Flinch bounced up and down in excitement. 'Oh, yes. Can we?'

Meg smiled. 'If you like.' She needed to be back home before her father got in from work – or rather from the pub. But that would be a good couple of hours yet. She led Flinch up the short flight of steps into the entrance hall of the gallery. The mirror maze was in one of the rooms off the hall, advertised by a large blackboard leaning against the wall beside the door.

Sitting at the little table outside the door to the maze was a wizened old lady. She was huddled up in a shawl and a mass of material that might have been a combination of dress, blouse and coat. From somewhere deep inside, curls of grey hair escaped. Meg caught a glimpse of deep-set dark eyes – pinpricks of black – as the woman looked up. She said nothing, but a gnarled hand emerged from what might have been a sleeve. It grasped the tin that was standing on the table and shook it just enough to make the coins inside clink against each other and the metal sides.

Flinch was looking apprehensively at Meg. The older girl tried to smile back, but she had to admit there was something unsettling about the old woman. Meg dropped her few coins into the tin, took Flinch's hand and led her quickly into the mirror maze. Behind her, Meg heard the old woman muttering. Whether it was thanks or disappointment at the amount Meg had put in the tin, she could not tell.

'I think she's a witch,' Flinch hissed as they entered the room.

'I think you might be right,' Meg said.

The mirror maze was dimly lit. Spotlights provided sudden pools of illumination, but the light did not seem to spread. This made it even more difficult to discern the shape of the room and the maze. There were mirrors everywhere. As soon as they stepped inside, the two girls found themselves standing in a forest of reflections of each other. Meg turned to Flinch, about to tell her to stay close. But when she reached out to take her friend's hand, her fingers grazed the smooth surface of a mirror. The dozens of Flinches round her laughed at the many startled expressions on the Megs' faces.

Flinch – the real Flinch – took Meg's other hand and together they made their way cautiously forwards. It was surprising how things that looked so real could be reflections, Meg thought. Several times she walked into a mirror without realising the path lay in another direction. The pools of light were a further distraction. What looked like a line of lights leading you onwards might turn out to be the reflection of other reflections of just a single light.

But while Meg found it difficult to navigate, having to feel her way along the mirrored walls as often as not, Flinch had no problem working out which way to go. The girls seemed to alternate between groans of frustration and nervous laughter. Meg found she was at once excited and amused at the challenge of getting round the maze, and at the same time she was fighting to keep herself from panicking – afraid they might be trapped in here for ever, going round in circles and chasing their own reflections until doomsday.

'How did you know that?' Meg demanded as

Flinch led her through what had seemed to be another mirror.

'It's easy,' Flinch told her. 'You look at the ceiling.'

That made no sense to Meg, but she looked up where Flinch was pointing. And suddenly she understood. It was so simple. If you looked at the real spotlights above, you could follow the beams of light with your eyes down to the ground. Then you knew which were real and which must be reflections.

Using Flinch's technique, they swiftly managed to find their way across the room. Meg was expecting the path to lead round the room and back to the entrance, or possibly to another exit door. But she was wrong. At the back of the room there was an open area. Close to the back wall, a semicircular line of mirrors was set up, angled so that, as you emerged into the area, they all threw back your reflection. Flinch and Meg both stared across at them and then collapsed in fits of giggles.

They were distorting mirrors. The Flinches and Megs that laughed back at them were all out of proportion. Some were short and fat, others strung out into thin stick-people. One Meg had an elongated neck, while there was a Flinch who seemed to consist merely of a head stuck on a pair of feet that sort of waddled forwards as she walked.

On the other side of the line of distorting mirrors was another opening into the maze – the route out again, Meg guessed.

'It'll be quicker getting out,' Flinch assured her. 'We know how to do it now.'

They spent a few minutes standing in front of each of the mirrors, looking and laughing at their weird reflections.

'What shall we do next?' Flinch asked as they finally started back through the maze. 'We've looked at everything again now. Except the apes.'

'Yes.' Meg nodded thoughtfully. 'I didn't much like the performing apes,' she admitted. 'But I'd like to take another look at them.'

'Why?'

'Because the man with them wasn't telling the truth.'

Flinch shrugged. 'He's a showman. He makes stuff up so you'll pay money.'

'Yes,' Meg agreed. 'But there was more to it

than that, I think. Anyway, I'd like to see the apes again. I just thought he was, well, dishonest.'

It was only a feeling – she could not be sure. She was not even certain really what it was she had felt as they watched the performance the previous evening. Perhaps she just didn't like the man.

'All right,' Flinch said.

They could see the door now, the huddled bundle of rags that was the old woman still sitting at the little table. Several people were coming into the maze, seeming to walk past and through the path that Meg and Flinch were on.

'I don't mind watching the monkeys,' Flinch was saying.

Meg made the mistake of heading straight for the doorway – and walked into a mirror. Flinch laughed, hiding her mouth behind her hand when Meg glared at her. But her amusement was revealed in several mirrors beside her.

'Do you think,' Flinch said when she'd finished giggling, 'that one of the apes might have escaped and hurt Elsie?'

'Then she would have been found,' Meg said. 'Unless the showman . . .' She paused.

'Did what?' Flinch wanted to know.

Meg sighed. 'Well, unless he paid her to go away and not mention it, or took her to the hospital or something.'

Unless he hid the body, she was thinking. But it seemed so improbable that she did not want to frighten Flinch with the thought.

Suddenly they were back in the entrance hall, having stepped between two mirrors and out of the maze.

'Let's go and see the creepy showman, then,' Flinch agreed, as they walked down the steps and out into the crisp night air. She nudged Meg and whispered loudly, 'Perhaps he hid Elsie's body.'

Although neither Art nor Jonny had any idea who he was, they were saved from being bought drinks by Old Toby.

It seemed as if Maurice was not going to take 'no' for an answer. Art and Jonny both protested that they didn't need another drink, but Maurice was determined to get his round in – and that included his new friends as well as the man with the moustache and Gladys.

He was just pushing his way towards the bar,

having promised he would return with a couple of full pints this time for Art and Jonny, when he paused. 'Hello,' he remarked loudly, 'what's up with Old Toby?'

Jonny turned, aware that Art was also craning to see what was happening closer to the bar. People were shuffling aside, looking down at the ground. Jonny wondered at first if someone had fainted. A nervous silence settled in the pub as more and more people seemed to register that something was amiss. Jonny stood up.

He could see now that Old Toby was not someone who had fainted or drunk too much and become ill. Old Toby was a dog. In fact, Jonny realised, he had seen what must be this same dog round the place before, out on the nearby streets. But he had never seen him like this.

Old Toby was a small terrier, although the way his hair was standing up made him look bigger than he was. Even across the room, Jonny could hear his growling and could see that his hair was standing up on end. The dog's mouth was open in a snarl and he let out an angry, aggressive bark.

'Never seen him like that before,' Gladys

said. She sounded worried, almost frightened.

Art was standing beside Jonny now. 'He's not usually *like* that,' Art said. He obviously knew Old Toby better than Jonny did. 'Something's upset him,' he murmured.

'So long as it isn't us,' Jonny replied.

He thought he was talking as quietly as Art, but as he spoke Old Toby's head swung round as if he had heard. The dog stared directly at Jonny, who took an instinctive step backwards.

Albert Norris appeared from behind the bar, looking puzzled as he approached his dog. He was talking quietly, trying to soothe it. But Jonny wasn't listening to what he said. Neither was Old Toby. The dog was stalking slowly forwards, eyes still fixed on Jonny, a line of viscous spittle escaping from his open jaw and hanging like a spider's thread to the floor.

As Norris finally reached down to try to pick him up, Old Toby hurled himself forwards – across the room and straight at Jonny. The dog was incredibly fast for his size and even Jonny had no time to turn and run. He took another step backwards, just as the dog launched himself from the floor – paws extended, claws out, aiming for

Jonny's neck. He seemed to be staring straight down the beast's throat.

'Sorry!' Art's shout distracted Jonny for a second. But only a second, because then Jonny's feet were kicked from under him and he fell backwards to the floor with a cry of surprise. He landed in time to see the dog go flying over his head, jaws closing on the space where his throat had been a moment earlier.

But his relief was short-lived. What seemed like only seconds later, the dog was back and bounding across the pub, once again with Jonny in his sights. Jonny lashed out with his foot as the dog reached him, but he missed. Old Toby had leaped over Jonny's foot and dived towards his other leg. Before Jonny – or anyone else – could reach the dog, he had clamped his mouth round Jonny's lower leg, snarling and shaking his head as he tried to rip through Jonny's trousers.

Art was grabbing at the dog, dragging him away. Albert Norris was shouting, helping Art, and eventually he managed to pull the dog clear. He wrapped his large fingers through the dog's brown leather collar and dragged him back. Then he carried the snarling, snapping creature away.

'I'll shove him in the coal shed till he calms down,' Norris shouted. 'Can't think what's got into him, daft dog. Still' – the landlord's voice was fading and other people were starting to talk again – 'he couldn't have done any harm. The last of his teeth rotted and fell out years ago. He can barely eat minced rabbit and gravy these days . . .'

'Are you all right?' Art helped Jonny to his feet.

Jonny's leg hurt like anything and he needed Art's help to limp to the door. 'I reckon that saved us from Maurice's drinks,' he said between gasps of pain.

Art gave a wry smile. 'Bit of a drastic solution, though.'

Once outside, Art helped Jonny to the edge of the pavement, where they both sat down on the cold ground. Jonny stretched out his leg and rubbed it. From behind them they could hear the pub returning to its normal level of noise. Across the street the other way, they could hear the sounds of the fair.

'That organ's still hammering away,' Art said.

'So's my leg.' Jonny pulled up his trouser leg to examine the damage. A streetlight above them cast a pale glow over the red beginnings of a nasty bruise, but the pain was starting to ease.

'At least he didn't break the skin,' Art said, carefully feeling round the slight swelling on Jonny's calf.

'Good job he's got no teeth.'

'Ye-es,' Art replied.

'What is it?' Jonny could hear the puzzlement in Art's voice. He sat up and leaned forward so he could examine the marks on his leg better. And immediately he saw what Art had seen. The skin was not broken. But the evidence was still there – the marks where Old Toby had bitten him. Two semicircles of indentations that had obviously been made by the dog's sharp teeth.

Teeth that everyone knew Old Toby no longer had.

The showman was finishing by the time that Meg and Flinch arrived. Maybe he would do another performance later in the evening, but for the moment he was roughly herding his apes back into their wheeled cage.

The girls stood for a while and watched him pushing and cajoling the massive animals. They seemed surprisingly docile and Meg guessed that they were used to it. They probably also knew what would happen if they disobeyed their master. It was no surprise to Meg to see that he had a long, heavy stick strapped to his waist and she could guess all too easily how it might be used.

'Where's the big one?' Flinch asked. 'The ape that does the sums and stuff?'

'I don't know.' Meg looked round. She could not see it anywhere. 'Maybe it's already in the cage, lying down or something?'

'Perhaps it's wandered off.' Flinch's eyes were large with apprehension. She looked round, as if expecting the gigantic ape to loom suddenly out of the night and hurl itself at them.

'I doubt it,' Meg said. But she was not as sure as she hoped she sounded. 'You stay here – you'll be quite safe with the showman sorting them out – and I'll check round the other side of the cage.'

Flinch nodded. But she was biting her lower lip, which meant she was nervous.

Meg touched the young girl on the arm. 'Won't be a minute,' she promised.

The showman's caravan all but blocked the street and Meg had to squeeze past. It would have been easy for Flinch, she thought. But if there was an ape wandering loose, then she did not want Flinch to have to face it alone. Actually, she thought, she did not want to face it herself.

Meg tried to convince herself that there was nothing to worry about. If one of the apes had escaped, the showman would have noticed. It was in his interests that they were all accounted for – for his act, and because if anyone did spot a stray ape, it would be pretty obvious where it had escaped from and whom to blame.

So Meg was almost certain that when she looked into the cage from the other side, she would be able to see the biggest of the apes, the 'Mighty Kong', lying quietly inside. But she was wrong. Had he moved? As she was coming round the back, had Kong gone to the front of the cage? Was Flinch even now watching the ape with amusement and wondering where Meg had got to as she stared at the cage from this side? That must be it, Meg decided, and she turned to go.

There was a figure standing behind her, partly hidden by the shadows of the buildings down the side of the street so that Meg could see only the outline, the silhouette of the enormous figure. It was keeping still, as if hoping that she would not see it, but it was obvious from the way she had stopped and stared as she tried to make out the shape that she had.

The figure stepped forwards into the grey evening light.

And Meg saw that it was the gigantic ape. Its hair seemed to gleam and its eyes were glowing with reflected light. The creature took another step towards Meg, arms hanging loose and long by its sides. It pulled itself upright from its crouched, almost hunched position and returned Meg's frightened stare, unblinking.

Meg swallowed, her throat dry. The best thing, she thought, was to back slowly away, making no sudden movements that might alarm the animal. She didn't like the way its jaw was moving, almost as if it was laughing at her. She took a step backwards, slowly, carefully.

Then the ape reached out a massive paw, the hairy fingers clutching the air, as if beckoning.

Slowly, carefully, Meg thought. Another step backwards.

Its jaw was moving again, she saw.

Hello,' the ape said.

And Meg screamed, turned and ran.

Arthur struggled and kicked, but the bearded man was holding him tight, pressing his arms into his sides. For several seconds, Arthur was too surprised to shout for help.

And several seconds was all it took for the man to bend Arthur over, forcing his head down, and propel him into the back of the car waiting at the kerb.

As Arthur sprawled across the seat, he realised that the man now had a problem. He seemed to realise it too. There was nobody else in the car, so how was he going to get to the driver's seat without allowing Arthur to escape?

When he spoke, the man's voice was a low grunt, forced out from behind the beard. 'Stay there,' he said. 'Your dad sent me to get you.'

'Yeah, right,' Arthur countered.

'Just stay there.'

The man was holding something. He slammed

the door shut and there was a dull click. With a stab of fright, Arthur suddenly knew that the car doors must be child-locked – they wouldn't open from the inside.

Now he did yell, hammering at the windows and wrenching the handle, but to no effect. He was trapped.

The driver's door unlocked – but none of the other doors did. The man was climbing in, reaching to push the key into the ignition. He was about to drive off – with Arthur in the car.

But then he was getting out again. Quickly. No – not getting out but falling out, caught off balance as he climbed in and sent sprawling into the road. At once, Arthur threw himself between the front seats of the car, rolling on to the driver's side and catching his ankle painfully on the gear stick in the process. He could see Sarah's hair flying round her head as she struggled to keep out of reach of the man, who was now sprawled on the ground. Then Arthur was out of the car, grabbing Sarah's hand and dragging her away, gasping his thanks.

They both ran until they were exhausted. Then they stood gasping and panting and laughing with relief.

'What was all that about?' Sarah said as soon as she had the breath.

He shook his head. 'Some nutter. I should have got the car number plate.'

Sarah was looking past Arthur, along the street. 'Now's your chance,' she said quietly.

Arthur turned in time to see the dark car barrelling down the street towards them. He could see a dark smudge through the windscreen that looked like a mass of beard. But the vehicle was moving too quickly for him to be sure. There was a screech of brakes and it swerved towards the pavement – towards Arthur and Sarah.

Arthur pushed Sarah away, diving in the opposite direction. The car glanced off the kerb, close to where they had been. It slowed as if about to stop. Then the driver seemed to think better of it and the car accelerated away, blue-grey exhaust smoke from the straining engine masking the number plate.

Chapter 3

'You're leaving early this morning,' Art's dad remarked.

'It's a nice morning, so I thought I'd take a walk.'

'A long-cut to school?' Dad seemed amused by the idea.

'Something like that.'

Dad nodded. 'Well, I'll see you later, then.' He waited until Art was at the door before adding, 'Got some work to finish up, have you?'

Art grinned. 'Might have,' he said. If Dad wanted to believe that, fine.

In fact, Art wanted to see someone. Sure enough, the old cellarman was sitting on an upturned barrel by the chute down into the cellar of the Dog and Goose. As usual at this time of the morning, he was tucking into a bacon sandwich before finishing hauling out the empty barrels for when the drayman passed later.

The cellarman's name was Bob. If he had another name, Art did not know it and suspected that no one else did either. Bob was old and wrinkled, with bushy white eyebrows and a handlebar moustache. What hair he had left was completely hidden under his cap. But his eyes were deep blue and alert with interest. His arms were weather-beaten and muscular under the brittle white hair. He gave no sign that he had seen anyone approach, but he nodded and mumbled a 'good morning' as Art passed.

Feigning surprise, Art pulled up another empty barrel and sat beside Bob. 'Didn't see you there,' he said.

Bob nodded thoughtfully and took another bite of sandwich. 'Course not,' he said a little indistinctly. 'Mind on other things, I expect.'

'Could be.' Although he had only just had breakfast, the smell of the bacon was making Art feel hungry.

'You're a good lad, Art Drake,' Bob said when he had finished eating. He folded up the greasy paper bag the sandwich had been in and stuffed it into his pocket. 'But whenever you stop by for a chat it's because you're after something. Always one for questions, aren't you?' He seemed amused rather than annoyed.

Art watched how Bob's face wrinkled and wondered vaguely if he would ever live to be that old. 'I have an enquiring mind,' he said, returning the man's smile.

'You've certainly got that. So what's today's question? Want to know if the Star and Garter is watering the pale ale again, do you?'

'I was just worried about Old Toby.'

Bob frowned. 'Old Toby? Why, what's up with him?'

'I thought you might tell me.'

'Seemed right as rain just now, poking about round the bins as usual.'

Bob pointed towards the alley that ran down the back of the pub. It was where the dustbins were kept and where Albert Norris stored old bottles and crates. Bob would be rolling the empty barrels down there when he had hauled them out of the cellar.

'There's a rumour that he attacked someone. In the pub. Last night,' Art added, seeing Bob's frown deepen into incredulity. 'You hadn't heard?'

'Not likely to neither.' He shook his head and laughed. 'Old Toby wouldn't hurt a fly. *Couldn't* hurt a fly, come to that.' He put two fingers to his mouth and let out a piercing whistle that made Art's ears ring. 'Oi, Toby. Here, boy. Here,' Bob called.

Old Toby emerged – eventually – from the alley. But while it was recognisably the same terrier, this was a very different dog from the one that had attacked Jonny the previous night. He looked smaller, older. His fur was lying flat and thin across his back, and he dragged one of his back legs when he walked. The long, grey hairs round Old Toby's mouth made it look as if the dog was growing a beard. Yet the collar was the same and the colouring of the fur. It was definitely the same dog.

The terrier limped painfully over to allow Bob to stroke and pet him. 'Wouldn't hurt a fly, would you, boy?' Bob repeated.

Art watched for a while as Bob leaned down to look into Old Toby's pale eyes, cradling the dog's head in his hands affectionately. He made to stroke him, ready to pull his hand away as soon as the dog turned savage.

But Old Toby was plainly too frail to object to the petting. As Bob moved to let him take over the petting, Art used the opportunity, carefully and hesitantly, to feel round the dog's mouth. He prised the jaw open, leaning forward to look inside.

What he saw was the pale pink of the dog's

gums. There were slightly darker patches where the skin had healed over the empty sockets – empty sockets where Old Toby's teeth had been. Long ago.

Bob watched with amusement as Art let him go and the dog limped away towards the door into the pub.

'No way he's going to attack anyone,' Bob said. He stood up and brushed the crumbs off his trousers. 'Anyway, there's enough rumours about young Elsie without starting any more about Old Toby.'

'And what do you think has happened to Elsie?' Art followed Bob as the old man rolled a barrel down the alley.

'Probably got a better offer from another pub. Or a hotel maybe.'

'Did she tell you that?'

'Always questions isn't it?' He let the barrel settle against the back wall of the alley. 'No, she didn't. I haven't seen Elsie since middle of last week. Lots of people seen her more recently than me, I expect. Ask them.'

'Like who?' Art wanted to know.

'Like him.' Bob was looking past Art and

nodded, touching his cap deferentially. 'Morning, Mr Sayers.'

'Morning, Bob.'

Art turned to see a man emerging from the back door of the pub. There was a small hallway inside the back door and steps led up to the two rooms above that were let out to guests. The man was well dressed and clean-shaven. He was tall and good-looking, his face long and thin and his hair perfectly parted and neatly combed. He was wearing a heavy grey overcoat and carrying his hat and gloves.

Seeing Art's interest, the man nodded and smiled. 'Morning,' he said again.

'Good morning,' Art replied.

'Young Art here is worried about Miss Elsie,' Bob said. Then, as if this ended the conversation, he turned and walked back out of the alley.

Mr Sayers did not move. 'We're all worried about Miss Elsie,' he told Art. 'I haven't seen her – indeed, I gather that no one has seen her – since last Friday. Are you a friend of hers?'

'Yes,' Art said. 'Well, a friend of a friend, you know.'

Sayers nodded, putting on his hat. 'Yes, a

pleasant girl. Quiet and efficient. Certainly I had no complaints about her work. My room has always been immaculate. So I doubt she would just run off.' He pulled on a glove, stretching out the fingers first to make it easier.

'Bob says she might have got a better job.'

Sayers nodded. 'Yes,' he said. 'Yes, I expect that's it. Well, nice to meet you, Art. I mustn't keep you.' He smiled politely, tipped his hat and walked briskly along the alley towards Cannon Street.

'Art?' Flinch asked as the two of them walked through the fair that evening.

'Yes?' He had bought her a stick of candyfloss and for a while that had kept her completely quiet. But now the candyfloss was gone and she was evidently keen to check on something. 'What is it?'

'Monkeys – like apes and Mighty Kong – well . . .' She paused, lips pursed together, before finishing in a rush, 'I mean, they can't really talk, can they?'

'No,' Art assured her, smiling. 'No, they can't. Meg just imagined it, that's all. She knows that. She told us that. She was a bit startled and someone spoke the other side of the cage just as she saw Mighty Kong.'

'She was spooked,' Flinch said. She grinned suddenly and widely. 'You should have seen her running back, should have heard her.'

Art laughed. 'I don't think Meg would agree. But yes, she still didn't want to see the apes tonight, did she?'

Meg and Jonny had gone instead to the Dog and Goose. They had all agreed earlier in the evening, back at the den, that having to resort to keeping watch on an old dog and group of performing apes was pretty ridiculous. But nobody had any better suggestions. So while Meg and Jonny waited outside the pub to see if Old Toby threw another fit, Flinch and Art were enjoying the fair.

'Do you want to see the mirror maze?' Flinch asked. 'It's really good.'

'I'm sure it is. But I want to check up on the apes first. Just to be sure there's nothing weird there.'

Flinch nodded. 'All right. Then can we have more chestnuts?'

The apes were in the middle of a routine. Two of them were swaying from side to side, while the huge Mighty Kong stood in between and clapped its hands. When the swaying dance was finished the two apes loped round with tins to collect money. Art was relieved to see that both were shackled to long chains that meant the crowd was out of reach of their huge paws. Not that they seemed to show any signs of being violent or aggressive.

While Flinch watched the Mighty Kong going through his sums and doing some juggling, Art took the opportunity to sneak a closer look at the cage. Meg was right, he quickly decided. If there was anything of interest to see, it must be round the other side, hidden from the public. Art was not really sure what he might find, but he was determined to look.

The performance was nearing its end and Art led Flinch away from the crowd. They didn't want to be caught refusing to pay again. Together they slipped past the showman's caravan into the dimly lit street beyond, then doubled back to the other side of the apes' cage.

'Look at that,' Flinch gasped.

Art could see at once what she was pointing at. One of the bars of the cage had been twisted out of shape, pulled sideways.

'Is that big enough for the monkeys to get out?'

'I don't know,' Art admitted, his voice barely audible above the applause from the other side of the cage.

'I could get through there,' Flinch said.

Art smiled. 'I'm sure you could. But that doesn't mean one of those big apes could. And I wouldn't suggest you try it. You might end up stuck in the cage with them.'

Flinch shuddered at the thought.

Art went up to the bar and took hold of it. 'What could have done this?' he wondered. 'These bars must be incredibly strong.' He pulled with all his might, leaning backwards and yanking as hard as he could. But the bar refused to budge.

As he pulled, a heavy weight came down on Art's shoulder. He turned quickly. Flinch was gone and the showman was standing behind him now, hefting the wooden stave in a very threatening manner.

'So, trying to steal my prize apes, are you?'

'No,' said Art quickly. 'I just saw the bar was bent and I wondered how that happened.'

'Did you now?' The showman smacked the stave into the palm of his hand with a solid-sounding thwack. 'I reckon I should call the coppers, see what they think.' He took a step towards Art and raised the club. 'Or maybe I'll just deal with this myself. 'Cause someone's been trying to steal my apes, bending the bars, trying to get into their cage. I doubt a kid like you could do it, but maybe you know who did.'

He took another step forwards and Art found himself pressed against the bars of the cage. A rough, dark hand appeared over his head and rubbed at his cheek. It stank and Art pulled away. But he could still feel the ape's paw curiously clawing at his back. Playful – for now.

'Well?' The showman's eyes narrowed to slits. 'You going to tell me or do I need to encourage you? Or maybe just put you in there with Goliath for a night or two to loosen your tongue, what do you think?'

Art was about to tell him what he thought, when there was an ear-piercing shriek from the other side of the cage. A child's scream split the air, making the showman look up abruptly.

'The monkeys are out!' a shrill voice squealed. 'Oh, quick, they're escaping and going mad.'

The showman glared at Art for a second, then he turned and ran back round the cage.

As soon as he was gone, Art breathed a sigh of relief. He tried to move away from the cage. But something grabbed his leg – a paw clutching at his ankle and dragging him back. With a screech of fright, Art pulled his leg away and turned in horror to see what was reaching for him.

It was a thin, grubby hand, a child's hand, beckoning at him from under the cage. 'Come on!' Flinch hissed. 'Quick, before he comes back.'

Art laughed out loud with relief and dived under the cage. He found Flinch crouching beside one of the large wheels. Oil had dripped from the axle and made a dark, sticky patch on the ground close by.

'I thought if I shouted his monkeys were escaping, he'd go to look,' she whispered proudly.

Art reached out and ruffled her hair. 'Well done,' he mouthed, then put his finger to his lips.

The showman's booted feet were visible, making their way back round the cage, looking again for Art. They heard his grunt of disappointment that the boy had gone, then the boots stamped off in the direction of his caravan.

Art and Flinch crawled out from their hiding place and ran quickly to lose themselves in the crowds at the fair.

It seemed like a typical evening at the Dog and Goose. Maybe there was a bit more business than usual, brought in by the nearby fair, but otherwise Jonny could see nothing out of the ordinary as he and Meg kept watch from across the street.

Meg, of course, was being sullen and wasted no opportunity to tell Jonny how awful it was that people spent so much time drinking. Jonny did not rise to the bait and eventually Meg admitted, 'I should be getting home soon.'

They had just seen Old Toby limping his way into and out of the alley behind the pub. He looked for all the world like a tired old pub dog, and nothing like the ferocious animal that had launched the attack on Jonny the night before. A few minutes after Old Toby emerged from the alley, an old man shuffled past, paused to peer into the darkness, then made his way down the alley as well. Probably seeing what he could scavenge out of the bins, Jonny thought.

'Well,' Jonny told her, 'I don't think anything much is likely to happen now. Have you got time to see if Art and Flinch are back at the den?'

She nodded, at exactly the same moment as a cry of surprise and fear came from somewhere close by.

'What was that?' Jonny said, his stomach turning over at the possibilities.

'Too close to be from the fair,' Meg said. She looked pale and drawn in the dim light.

As if to confirm this, there was another cry – this time a shriek of absolute terror. They both realised where it had come from.

'The alley,' Meg said.

Jonny was already on his way. Despite his fear, he raced across the road. But at the entrance to the dark passageway, he hesitated.

'Oh, come on,' Meg urged, catching up. She pushed past him and ran into the alleyway. Jonny sighed and followed.

There was a little light spilling out from the

grimy back windows of the pub. Enough to illuminate the scene in front of them. The old man they had seen was up against the wall of the alley, opposite the back door of the pub. He was struggling, flailing, trying to shout again. But the small, hunched figure that had pushed him up against the wall had a hand tight over his mouth. The old man's grey eyes were wide with fear. A knife glinted as it caught the light, and then Meg screamed.

The hunched figure turned abruptly at the sound. Its face was masked in shadow, but its shape was that of a deformed, shrunken dwarf. It lurched back from the old man, who collapsed to the ground and staggered down the alleyway towards Meg and Jonny.

'Grab him!' Meg shouted, running to help the old man.

The misshapen figure all but brushed past Meg as she ran. Jonny watched in horror as it approached him. He reached out half-heartedly, wondering if it still had the knife. But the figure broke suddenly into a stumbling, shuffling run and was past him before he could react.

He spared a glance for Meg. She was

kneeling beside the old man, helping him to his unsteady feet, checking he was all right. Jonny swallowed and took a deep breath. Then he turned and ran back along the alley. He could catch up with the figure easily. Probably he could hold him until Meg got the police or he managed himself to call for help. He remembered the glint of the knife and tried to push it to the back of his mind.

At the end of the alley, Jonny looked first one way, then the other. He thought he would easily be able to spot the shambling figure on the pavement. But the street seemed deserted. The sounds of the pub mingled with the more distant noises from the fair. Where could the old man's attacker have gone? With a gut-wrenching feeling of icy terror, Jonny realised there was only one place it could be – behind him. If the attacker had simply stopped at the end of the alley and ducked into the shadows by the pub wall . . .

Even as the thought occurred to him, even as his blood went cold and he turned slowly to face the shadows, even as he saw Meg helping the old man to steady himself at the far end of the alleyway, Jonny felt a hand descend on his shoulder and grip it tightly.

The ground seemed to glow in the moonlight. The pallid light of the moon and the stars was reflected by the tight-packed snow as it crunched under Arthur's feet. The air was crisp and cold and he could feel the tips of his ears glowing as the evening set in and the temperature dropped still further.

It had been after six o'clock when they arrived and snowing quite heavily. Arthur's first glimpse of Montgrave House through the snow-laden trees had not done anything to dispel his fears. He was sure that the hotel would turn out to be stuffy and boring and in the middle of nowhere. Seeing the front of the eighteenth-century house set back in its snow-covered parkland, several of the upper windows boarded over and the stonework visibly crumbling, served only to confirm his suspicions.

'It's a dump,' Arthur said quietly enough for his dad to pretend he had not heard.

They had spent much of the journey in silence, Arthur still not sure he had done the best thing by telling his dad about the man who had tried to drive him off. Dad had insisted on filing a police incident report, of course. Arthur had even had to give a statement. Now that it was over and done with, it all seemed like a lot of fuss, though he still shivered when he remembered being locked inside the car.

There were several cars parked on the snowy gravel driveway to the side of the house. Dad and Arthur huddled into their coats and carried their bags round to the main entrance. There was no one at the desk marked 'Reception' and they had to ring a bell.

Eventually an annoying young man with greasy black hair and a habit of rubbing his hands together appeared. He immediately made it clear that he was in charge and they were expected to enjoy their stay. He made no mention of how they came to be there and Arthur wondered if he knew they weren't paying. Or perhaps he treated all the guests with the same dismissive attitude.

More polite, but to Arthur's mind more unsettling, was Mrs Trefusis. The man who had greeted them and announced himself the manager was her nephew, Christopher Peters. Mrs Trefusis, as she told Arthur and Dad in a quiet but intense voice, was the owner. She was an elderly lady with steel-grey hair and long, thin features that made it look as if her face had been squeezed between bookends. She sat upright and aristocratic in a wheelchair, a tartan blanket over her knees. Her nurse – a formidable middle-aged woman with severe dark hair tied tight in a bun – stood stoically holding the handles of the chair, ready to wheel Mrs Trefusis away at the slightest hint of anything untoward.

Seeing Arthur glancing at the woman, Mrs Trefusis leaned forwards slightly. 'Don't mind Miss Napier, young man,' she said, stressing the 'young' for some reason. 'You are Arthur Drake, aren't you?' she added, although Dad had already introduced them. 'Yes. Yes, I thought you were.' She waved her hand in the air, rather like the Queen acknowledging her subjects, and Miss Napier interpreted this as a signal to move on.

'I shall see you at dinner at eight,' Mrs Trefusis called back to them as she was wheeled along the hallway and back into the dark depths of Montgrave House.

It was at this point that Arthur decided he needed to get some air. As soon as they had dumped their bags in the room – a damp-smelling wood-panelled chamber on the first floor – Arthur told Dad he'd see him in time for dinner.

'Off exploring?' Dad asked.

'Just going to have a look out in the grounds, before it gets any darker,' Arthur said. He hesitated. 'You can come with me if you like.'

But Dad seemed to catch the hesitancy in the offer. 'You run along. I'll unpack. And I need to call in and check my messages.' He pulled out his mobile and frowned. 'No network. That's typical, isn't it?' He looked round. 'And no phone in the room.'

Arthur remembered seeing an old coin-box pay phone in the entrance hall. He mentioned it to Dad. 'You can call Scotland Yard on that.'

'I need a touch-tone to get my messages, though. That probably won't do.' Dad sighed. 'Never mind, we'll worry about that later. Go on now, if you must. But be back in time to get ready for dinner.'

Having been outside for half an hour, Arthur was cold yet reluctant to go back indoors. He didn't like the place, he decided. It wasn't just that he had expected it would be awful – it *was* awful. And he was stuck here for the whole weekend. He kicked at the snow in front of him, sending it up in misty clouds of frustration.

There was a small wooded area to the side of the driveway and, as he walked back towards the house, Arthur became aware that a figure was watching him. There was a man – tall and thin – standing at the edge of the wood, silhouetted in the moonlight. Arthur paused, looking straight at him. He was so still he might be a statue.

Arthur had almost decided that he *was* a statue, when the man moved, walking slowly across the snow-covered lawn.

'Good evening,' Arthur called out as the man approached. 'Are you staying here?'

The man shook his head. He had short sandy-coloured hair and was clean-shaven. He was wearing jeans and a T-shirt despite the cold. 'I work here,' he replied.

'Arthur Drake. I'm staying at the hotel.' He offered his hand, but the man did not seem to see it.

'I'm Bill McNeil. Groundsman.'

'Is that the same as being a gardener?'

The man nodded. He looked to be in his thirties, but his face was cratered like the surface of the moon. 'Gardener, chauffeur, general dogsbody. Been here long?'

'Just arrived,' Arthur admitted.

Bill McNeil nodded. 'Be leaving soon, I expect.'

'We're just here for the weekend.'

'You might decide to leave early.' He sounded hopeful.

'Why?'

Bill McNeil shrugged. 'Because of the snow. Roads will be treacherous if it keeps up. You don't want to be stuck here.'

That was true enough, Arthur thought. But before he could say so, the man had turned and walked away, back towards the wood.

When Arthur returned to the hotel there was another car parked next to Dad's. A young man was struggling from it to the main doors with two heavy suitcases and Arthur went to help him.

'Oh, thanks.' The man seemed surprised and cautious. He looked round, as if to check no one was watching, as he and Arthur manhandled the suitcases towards the hotel.

'I'm Arthur,' Arthur said, thinking that he seemed to have been introducing himself all evening. 'I'm staying here with my dad,' he added, in case the man thought he was one of the staff, sent out to help with the luggage.

'Oh, right.' The man put his suitcase down for a moment to get a better grip. 'Er, Smith,' he said. 'Here for the weekend. With, er, my wife.' He said it quickly, as if it was a secret, then hauled the suitcase up again and staggered onwards.

Dad was waiting outside the door, hands in his pockets, watching Arthur with amusement as he struggled with the suitcase.

'I'm not late, am I?' Arthur said.

'No. Just thought I'd get some air as well, before dinner.' Dad started down the steps. 'Here, let me help.'

Mr Smith was standing beside Arthur now and they both paused as Dad walked down the front steps towards them. Dad blinked, like he had something in his eye. He brushed absently at his shoulder, then frowned. He glanced down at his hand and then up at the sky. Suddenly he gave a cry of warning and hurled himself down the steps.

As he leaped, Arthur's dad stretched his arms wide, wrapping one round Arthur's chest, the other round Mr Smith. His weight and momentum sent all three of them flying down the steps to land in a tangled heap at the bottom. The snow, mercifully, cushioned the fall, but Arthur was left gasping for breath.

'What in heaven's name . . .' Mr Smith started to say.

Arthur just gaped. Halfway down the steps, a huge lump of stone crashed to the ground. It exploded into fragments, sending the heavy suitcase flying.

'Good grief,' Smith said, his voice quavering. 'I was standing just there.'

Dad picked himself up and helped Arthur to his feet.

'Yes,' said Arthur, his own voice also shaking. 'So was I.'

Chapter 4

Jonny nearly jumped out of his skin and Art stifled a laugh.

'What's up with you?' he asked.

'Don't do that.' Jonny shrugged Art's hand off his shoulder. 'I nearly died!' He breathed out heavily, then he too laughed. 'I thought you were the Hunchback of Cricklewood.'

'Very likely.'

'He was here,' Jonny insisted, to Art's amazement. 'Attacked that old man.' He pointed back down the alley to where Meg was talking to an old man who looked rather shaken. 'We heard him shout, got there and the hunchback ran off.'

'Is the old man all right?'

'Seems to be,' Jonny said.

'Where did the hunchback go?' Art demanded.

'I lost him. Disappeared. Thought he might have slipped round behind me.'

'And that's why you jumped when I tapped you on the shoulder,' Art realised.

'He had a knife,' Jonny said. 'Though he might have dropped it. I don't know.'

As they spoke, both boys were looking round to see where the mysterious hunchback might have gone. Meg joined them as the old man shambled off into the night, muttering and shaking his head.

'He'll be fine once he's over the shock. I have to get home,' Meg said.

'Yes, well, there's not a lot of point in any of us hanging around here,' Art decided.

Meg set off towards home, while Art and Jonny went the other way – back towards the den to check that Flinch was all right after the run-in with the showman and his apes. They had almost reached the old carpet warehouse at the bottom end of the street when Jonny stopped abruptly.

'There he is!' he cried out, pointing across the road.

On the opposite pavement, keeping to the shadows, was a small figure. The glow of a streetlamp caught it for a second, throwing a distorted shadow against the wall behind. A hunched, misshapen figure, short and stooped, shuffling purposefully along.

'Quick!' Art was already at the kerb, looking both ways as he got ready to run after the figure.

Opposite him, the figure looked up, realised it had been spotted and quickened its awkward pace.

Jonny raced past, but Art grabbed him by the collar, dragging him back as a tram swept past them right in front of Jonny's nose. It slowed, the driver ringing the bell in warning. As soon as the tram had rattled by, Jonny was off, Art close on his heels. They reached the other side of the road and looked around them in astonishment.

There was nowhere to hide, no entranceway to duck into, no doors or windows on this stretch of road. But the pavement was deserted – the figure had gone.

'That's not possible,' Jonny gasped. 'I lost him before, but he'd hidden in the shadows or something.' He turned a full circle, his arms outstretched. 'But here – there's nowhere he could have gone.'

Art had to agree. The street was deserted. There wasn't even any traffic, save for the tram now turning out of the other end of the street. Its bell rang forlornly in the night, as if to remind people it existed.

'Of course,' Art said out loud. 'The tram.' He

was already running, Jonny keeping pace with him – not overtaking, as he didn't know where Art was going or what he meant. 'He got on the tram as it went past, when it slowed down,' Art shouted. 'We have to catch that tram!'

Jonny took off like a rocket.

The tram was not moving quickly, but it had a good head start. It disappeared round the corner, Jonny in pursuit. Art was amazed to see that Jonny was actually gaining on the tram as it slowed to take the corner. But their only hope, Art thought, was that the tram would stop before they lost sight of it.

He was out of breath by the time he reached the corner. He expected to find Jonny on his way back to meet him, disappointed at having lost his race. But the tram had stopped just fifty yards down the street and Jonny was haring towards it.

It pulled out again before he arrived. But rather than chasing after it, Jonny skidded to a halt. And as he approached, Art could see why. There were two trams. One had pulled out and the other was still stopped to let passengers off. Which was the one that had passed them – the one the hunchback had boarded?

Jonny was turning and waving, pointing at the stopped tram as he ran after the one that was pulling away and starting down the road. Incredibly, it looked as if he might catch it.

Forgetting about Jonny for the moment, Art concentrated on catching the other tram before it moved on. He waved and shouted, hoping the driver or conductor might see him and wait. But they didn't. The tram was off again, noisily and ponderously pulling away, wheels squealing as they gripped the rails. Art hurled himself forwards in a last desperate attempt to reach it, running with his arm outstretched to try to grab the pole at the back, by the narrow staircase to the upper deck.

Ignoring the thumping and rasping in his chest and his throat, and not daring to think what might happen if he missed, Art took a running jump. His hand closed on the pole, but his feet skidded and slid as he was dragged along. He struggled to hold on, felt the tram increasing speed, saw the ground spinning past in a blur beneath him. He swung his other hand round, scrabbling for a grip. Finally he managed and hauled himself on to the tram, gasping with the effort.

'Ain't no call for that,' the conductor told him. He was watching with a mixture of amusement and disapproval. 'Where to?'

Art had no idea where the tram was going, let alone how far he wanted to travel. And, he realised as he hesitated, he had no money to pay for a ticket either. He looked round, hoping for inspiration.

But what he saw made his stomach lurch. Ahead of them he could see Jonny, unable to catch the other tram and slowing to a disappointed halt at the side of the road. Behind the tram, Art could see the group of passengers that had just disembarked as they walked off, going their different ways along the street.

One of them was a small hunched figure that kept to the shadows, lurching its way back towards Cannon Street.

The tram slowed for a corner and on an impulse Art grinned at the conductor.

'Sorry,' Art said. 'Wrong tram.' And he jumped.

As he flew through the air, two things struck Art. One was that this was a very bad idea. The other was Jonny.

Johnny had been racing towards the tram and,

as Art jumped off, he was jumping on. They met in a tangle of arms and legs and went spinning into the gutter. Amazingly, Jonny broke Art's fall without seeming to break any bones of his own. The two of them eventually came to a gasping halt and picked themselves up.

'Sorry,' Art said.

'I missed the other tram,' Jonny said, and they sat on the kerb, fighting for breath. 'He must be on that.'

Art shook his head, struggling to get the words out. 'No . . . No . . . Got off my tram. Saw him. Heading back the way we came.'

'So he thinks he's given us the slip,' Jonny said a few minutes later as they trotted along after the hunchback. 'Maybe he *did* drop his knife in the alley.'

'Wants to retrieve the evidence,' Art agreed. 'It's possible. Or perhaps he lives down there somewhere.'

They caught sight of the figure as they approached the pub once more. And again it was slipping into the alleyway behind the Dog and Goose.

'It's a dead end,' Art whispered to Jonny,

though there was no way the figure could hear them. 'We've got him.'

'Careful,' Jonny warned, tugging at Art's sleeve. 'If he *has* got a knife . . .'

Art nodded. 'There's two of us and he can't be far away.' He sighed. 'We should have asked on the tram, got a description, found out if anyone recognised or knew him. Still, never mind. It's too late now.'

The only light came from the windows in the back of the pub. Jonny and Art made their way cautiously along the alley, checking every shadow, every patch of darkness. They peered behind the rubbish bins and the empty barrels. They kicked aside old crates and boxes.

It was only when they had almost reached the back door of the pub that Art realised they were being watched. A figure stood in the darkness of the doorway and, as they approached, it stepped out into the light.

'Looking for something?' the figure asked.

Jonny gave a high-pitched gasp of fear and surprise. Art breathed out a sigh of relief.

'Mr Sayers.' He recognised the tall man standing in front of them.

'It's Art, isn't it?' Sayers walked slowly towards them. 'We met this morning, I remember.'

'That's right, sir. This is my friend Jonny.'

'Hello,' Jonny said weakly.

'Have you lost something?' Sayers asked. 'I was watching you. You seemed to be looking for something. Maybe you dropped it this morning when you were with Bob?'

'We thought . . .' Art wasn't sure quite what to say, how much to tell the man. 'We've lost a friend of ours. We thought he came down the alley.'

Sayers smiled. 'Think he's hiding from you, do you?' He set off towards the end of the alley, brushing past them. 'Well, he isn't down here. I was putting my gloves on when I saw you two arrive. There was nobody ahead of you. I'd have seen them.' He paused at the end of the alley, touching his hat politely by way of farewell. 'Good luck with your game.' Then he was gone.

Art arrived home just a few minutes before his father. It was long enough for him to get his breath back and give the impression he had been in for a while.

'We went to the fair again,' he said. 'Jonny and Meg helped an old man who was being attacked by a hunchback.'

He expected Dad to laugh at him or at least express disbelief. But instead he sighed and shook his head. 'Not another one,' he said.

'Another hunchback?'

'Another attack. There have been a few recently.'

'Really?' Art tried not to sound too excited. 'Any clues?'

'This hunched figure is seen,' Dad told him. 'But then he just seems to vanish. Into thin air.'

'Not much chance of catching him, then,' Art joked.

But Dad didn't laugh. He was rubbing his eyes and yawning. 'Oh, there's a theory going round as to who it is.' He gave a snort of derision and Art guessed it was not a theory his father had much time for. 'Daft if you ask me, but it's the last person anyone would think of.'

'That's often the case,' Art said, wondering who it might be.

Dad was already on his way upstairs when he answered, his voice floating down to Art. 'Yes,

this suspect is an expert at vanishing into thin
air . . .'

There seemed to be little distinction between staff
and guests at dinner. Neither was there much
choice – no menu, just a couple of main courses to
choose between. It really was, Arthur thought, like a
seedy, run-down country house.

Mr Smith was there, together with his wife,
who was small and pretty and quiet and looked
much younger than her husband. Whereas Mr Smith
seemed to take every opportunity to tell everyone
how he had just nearly been killed and what a lucky
escape it was and how he had Mr Drake to thank
for saving his life, Mrs Smith said almost nothing.

There was one other guest – a Mr
Huntingdon. He was a rather portly man who
seemed to be constantly sweating. His dark hair had
receded so far that Arthur thought if he watched he
might see it disappear completely by the end of the
meal. He wore an ill-fitting suit and tried to hide the
fact that his top shirt button wouldn't do up by

having a huge knot on his tie. But the tie kept slipping, which allowed his neck to bulge out. This somehow seemed appropriate, as above it he had a bulbous red nose and his eyes bulged as if trying to escape from his head. He was constantly looking round, listening to the conversation, examining the cutlery, inspecting the food . . . At one point he even lifted the tablecloth so as to peer underneath at the polished wooden table.

Mr Peters also ate with them, taking every opportunity to say what a lovely meal he was having and how good the service was. This counterpointed Mrs Trefusis's views, which seemed to be the opposite. She sat in her wheelchair at the head of the table and wasted no opportunity to berate Miss Napier for her slack service or the quality and temperature of the food. It seemed that Miss Napier was waitress and cook as well as nurse to Mrs Trefusis. She did not reply to the jibes and comments, but her battle-weary expression said it all.

Arthur himself said as little as possible. Dad seemed to have a similar survival strategy, and Arthur could tell he was not counting the holiday a total success.

At one point, just after the main course arrived, Dad leaned over and whispered to Arthur, 'Don't break your teeth on the peas.'

Arthur carefully tried a forkful of peas. They were hard as stones and rolled round his mouth like marbles as he tried to swallow them without laughing. The cabbage, by way of contrast, was so overcooked and soggy that it almost fell apart when he stuck his fork in, and dripped water all the way to his mouth. There was some meat too, but it was impossible to tell what it was supposed to be.

Mr Peters was once again explaining how good the meal was, and showing every sign of believing himself, when Arthur noticed the scars. At the top of the table, Mrs Trefusis was sighing and making the point that nobody – particularly Miss Napier – had passed her the gravy. She hauled herself as upright in her wheelchair as she could and reached down the table, past the oblivious Mr Smith.

Arthur watched her gnarled fingers clawing towards the gravy boat. It was too far away for him to reach either, but he wondered if he should get up and walk round the table to fetch it for her. Or would she think that rude – that he was drawing attention to her disability? But it was too late to pretend he had not noticed, for her piercing grey eyes were fixed on him even as she reached forwards.

Noticing at last what was happening, Mrs Smith muttered something inaudible and passed the gravy boat to Mrs Trefusis. And as the old lady took it, Arthur saw that the act of stretching had caused the long sleeves of her blouse to pull back, exposing her wrists. Her left wrist was wrinkled and mottled, as he might have expected, given her age and complexion. But her right wrist looked as if the flesh had been scooped out and the skin then stretched tight over the hole left behind. Tributaries of dead tissue ran like roots into the main scar – as if the fire that must have burned her so badly had splashed and spat while it attacked her arm.

Arthur looked away quickly, pushing the remains of the floppy cabbage to the side of his plate.

The morning was crisp, with a hint of snow in the air. Arthur felt as if he had not slept at all. The bed was so hard it was like lying on the bare boards of the floor. His dad was snoring contentedly at seven o'clock when Arthur finally gave up, pulled on his clothes and slipped out of the room.

The house seemed deserted and Arthur tiptoed so as not to disturb anyone else. He found a dusty library on the ground floor opposite the dining room, and a drawing room where faded leather furniture was gathered round as if for a cosy chat. But when he tested one of the large armchairs, it was as hard and uncomfortable as the bed. The leather was worn shiny with age and use.

Breakfast was not until eight-thirty and there was nothing to suggest that anyone was preparing it yet. Without really thinking about it, Arthur found he was on his way back upstairs. But rather than return to his room, he decided to go up another flight and see what was on the top floor of the house.

Nothing very much, was his first thought. The stairs arrived at the end of a corridor. Arthur could see rooms off to either side. Maybe this was where the staff lived, though he was sure Mrs Trefusis would be based on the ground floor. Certainly there was no sign of a lift.

Arthur turned to go back downstairs, and as he turned he noticed that there was another, narrower flight of stairs rising again. It led up to a wooden door. An attic perhaps?

The door was bolted. So Arthur drew back the bolts and pushed. The door creaked and complained but swung open. Immediately he felt cold. Which was not surprising, he realised, as the door led on to the roof of the house. He emerged into a gully between two of the peaked roofs. It was lined with lead, sloping gently down to the front of the house, where small holes allowed the rain to run out into the main gutter.

There was a low wall at the end, the top of the stonework cut like battlements. Several of the upright stones were missing and, peering cautiously over, Arthur saw that he was directly above the front door. In one place the ragged exposed stonework where there had once been an upright was not as weathered as the rest of the wall. The stone was pale and clean. With a jolt, Arthur realised this was where the lump of stone had fallen from the previous evening – the stone that had almost hit him.

Examining the wall, Arthur found that most of the masonry was in a poor state of repair. It was really not very surprising that lumps of stone had crumbled and fallen away. It was just bad luck that he had been underneath when it had happened.

Checking his watch, Arthur started to make his way back along the gully. As he reached it, the door started to open, creaking on its rusty hinges. Instinctively, Arthur ducked behind the door, so that as it opened he was hidden from view. He heard heavy breathing. A shadow fell across the tiled roof beside him – hunched and misshapen.

His heart pounding, Arthur risked a quick look round the side of the door. Standing in the gully, one hand still on the door and wheezing as he caught his breath, was Mr Huntingdon. He was bending over, so as to breathe more easily. His shadow was further distorted by the angle of the roof. Arthur saw him straighten up and look along the gully. Then he sighed and stepped back inside, closing the door behind him.

Arthur waited, holding his breath. What was the man doing? Maybe he was just looking round, like Arthur was. But he had not seemed interested in exploring the gully and seeing where it went. Almost as if he was checking on something close to the door.

Not that it mattered, Arthur decided. Then he looked down, where Mr Huntingdon had been looking, and he saw that beside the door – the other side from where Arthur had hidden – was a bucket. In the bucket, where Huntingdon must have seen them – assuming he had not been checking they were there anyway – were a heavy hammer and a large, blunt chisel.

Innocent enough in themselves, they were probably the sorts of tools you would need to set about repairing the stone wall. But they were also, Arthur realised, exactly what you would need if you wanted to break off one of the stone uprights. Break it off and send it crashing down on to the steps below.

His blood running even colder as he thought through the implications, Arthur turned the door handle and pulled. But the door did not open. It barely moved within its frame. Mr Huntingdon had bolted it behind him and Arthur was trapped on the roof.

Chapter 5

Although they kept watch on the apes at the fair and on the Dog and Goose for the rest of the week, by the weekend the Cannoniers had learned nothing new. Art had been going to suggest they spend Saturday and Sunday in further investigations, but the others seemed so despondent at the lack of progress that he relented and instead they spent most of Saturday at the fair.

Flinch delighted in showing Art and Jonny round the mirror maze, and before long they were laughing and joking and walking into reflections of themselves and each other. Meg spent the time looking round the rest of the small art gallery and said she had enjoyed herself, though she said it without a hint of a smile.

Jonny was busy with his family on the Sunday. Meg spent the day helping her mother at home. Art's father had the day off, and while Art managed to see Flinch at the den for an hour in the afternoon he otherwise spent the time at home. He enjoyed helping in their small back garden, and he laughed when Dad threatened to oil the squeaking front gate and then didn't get round to it. As always.

So on Monday evening, the Invisible Detective was able to offer no information about what had happened to the missing Elsie. He said that investigations were ongoing and promised to inform his audience as soon as anything new came to light.

Apart from this admission of failure, Art thought the session was going well. He sat in the huge armchair, all but smothered by the enormous overcoat, and allowed his hand to venture out and punctuate his words every now and then with a gesture. He was enjoying himself, in his element and knowing his friends were nearby. To help matters further, the barrel organ had been moved to another street, which was a great relief.

'Are there any more questions for this evening?' Art asked, keeping his voice deep and authoritative.

The voice that replied was even deeper, booming round the room and echoing off the bare floorboards. 'I should like to ask about the Hunchback of Cricklewood, if I may.'

There was something familiar about the voice, Art thought. As if it was someone he knew or at least had met. This was not unlikely, given that most of the audience would be local. But he was sure it was not someone who regularly attended the sessions or rather not someone who often asked the detective for advice or help.

'What in particular are you enquiring about?' Art – as Brandon Lake – asked.

'Well, is it true that a hunchback has been seen in these parts? Is it true he's responsible for attacking several people? And if it is, what are your opinions and thoughts, Mr Lake?' The questioner paused before adding significantly, 'Who do you think the culprit really is?'

Art was none the wiser about the motive behind the questions. Perhaps it was just understandable concern, but the voice had sounded more challenging than anxious. 'May I ask your own interest, sir?' Art responded.

The reply was offhand, almost casual. 'Just a concerned citizen. No real interest any more than anyone else.'

'I see.'

Art was working out his reply when something fluttered towards him, just visible in the dim light. A slip of paper dancing on the end of a thin string – a message flicked across to him by Jonny on the fishing line. Art unhooked the paper and quickly read the message, angling it so it caught the light.

'There is no evidence, no actual evidence,' Art said as he scrawled a reply, 'that the so-called Hunchback of Cricklewood even exists. Far less that he is now at large in the Cannon Street area.' There was a general sigh of disappointment at this. But the audience stilled again as Art went on, 'However, I can reveal to you that a figure answering the general description of the Hunchback of Cricklewood has been sighted in the area by several very reliable witnesses.'

'Have they informed the police?' the deep, booming voice asked abruptly.

Art was just reattaching the paper to the fish hook. He tugged gently on the line to let Jonny know there was a reply. 'Er, no,' he said. 'But a hunched figure did attack an old man in the alley behind the Dog and Goose last week.'

'Behind my pub?' Art did recognise Albert Norris's scandalised voice. 'No one told me about it.'

'The gentleman concerned was, I believe, rummaging through your rubbish at the time,' Art said. This caused some amusement, judging by the noise from behind him. 'Perhaps he was hoping to find something valuable. Or at any rate edible.'

'He should have come in the pub like everyone else,' Norris grunted.

'I think he might agree with you, in the light of subsequent events,' Art agreed. 'Does that answer the gentleman's question for now? Needless to say, I will pass on any further information that becomes available to me.'

'Very kind,' the deep voice said. 'It'll do for now, thank you.'

Jonny watched the large, dark shape of the man who had asked about the hunchback. Meg's message to Art had been that the man was lying, at least about the motive behind his questions. The reply from Art had been clear and short and was obviously intended for Jonny:

FOLLOW HIM WHEN HE LEAVES.

As the man turned, Jonny could see that he wore a hat pulled down low. His cheeks were fuzzy with a mass of whiskers. He was tall and broad, and Jonny hoped he could follow him without being spotted. The man was pulling up a muffler to cover his mouth and chin, so that only his eyes would be visible once he was out in the evening light. The silhouette moved as the man made his way slowly towards the back of the room.

Trusting that no one was looking, Jonny slipped from behind the curtains and followed him through the audience. He trod on someone's foot and mumbled an apology, keeping his head down and making as quickly as he could for the stairs. The man would surely notice if Jonny followed him out. So he wanted to get down the stairs and out of the building first.

Once he was at the stairs, Jonny descended quickly, taking them two at a time. He dashed across the road and watched from the shadows of a doorway as the man stepped out into the light cast by a nearby streetlamp. He looked even bigger in the open, his shape blotting out the door behind him as he too crossed the road.

At first, Jonny thought the man had seen him. But he stopped on the pavement close by and turned to watch the doorway – just as Jonny had done. He was checking that he was not being followed, Jonny realised. Just as well Jonny had got out first.

Satisfied that all was well, the man set off briskly along Cannon Street in the direction of the Victoria Embankment. Jonny slipped out from his cover and followed, keeping as close as he dared. Twice the man stopped abruptly and turned to look behind. But each time he seemed satisfied and continued on his way. Whoever he expected to be after him, it did not seem to be a young dark-haired boy.

Before long they were walking beside the river. The man still kept his face all but covered with his scarf and hat, and Jonny hung back. The Embankment was wide and fairly quiet, so it was easy to follow without seeming to. Easy to keep the man in sight. As they made their way round towards Whitehall, Jonny became more and more convinced that he had seen the man before. There was something about his manner, about the way he walked, about the very size of him and the whiskers that Jonny had spotted sprouting from the man's cheeks . . . It was not someone he knew well, but someone he had met briefly or seen around.

It was not until the man turned off the Embankment and started along Northumberland Avenue that Jonny realised where he might be going. And it was not until he turned again and went into a large building that Jonny remembered where he had seen the man before.

The building was in Great Scotland Yard and it was the headquarters of the Metropolitan Police. It was the building where Art's father, Detective Sergeant Peter Drake, worked.

Pausing in the doorway, the man had turned to take one last look round before going inside. He pulled his scarf away from his face to reveal his impressive grey moustache and whiskers. He took off his hat to reveal a head that was by contrast almost completely bald. He nodded, as if pleased with himself, and went into the building.

He was, Jonny now realised, Inspector Gilbertson – Sergeant Drake's superior in the police force.

Heaving and tugging on the door did no good at all. It was bolted fast. Arthur thought about putting his shoulder to it, but as the door opened towards him, that would mean he was trying the break the frame, not the bolt.

He concentrated instead on examining the door. The wood was, ironically, in good repair. If it had been looked after as well as the wall at the end of the gully, Arthur could probably have simply pulled it apart. But it was solid and strong. Snow was starting to fall now. Large flakes glistened and shone in the morning sunlight as they drifted down. He could feel them colliding coldly with his cheeks and melting in his hair.

Arthur tried to remember how large and strong the bolt was on the other side. There was a slight gap between the door and the frame, so he could just make out the dark shape of the bolts drawn across – two of them, one at the top and one at the bottom. They looked pretty firm and secure. He shivered, swinging his arms round his chest to try to keep warm. He did not dare stamp his feet for fear of going through the lead and the roof. He might be desperate to get back inside, but he wasn't yet prepared to fall through the ceiling and probably down the main staircase to do it.

Back at the other end of the gully, Arthur leaned out as far as he dared to look over and down. There was nobody in sight to whom he could call for help and it was much too far to risk trying to climb down. Even if the brickwork and stone had been well maintained. As it was, they would probably crumble away as soon as he put any weight on them.

Arthur ran his hand across the rough, flaking surface of the piece of wall where the stone had fallen away, slapping at it in frustration. Should there be chisel marks if someone had hacked and levered the stone out? Or perhaps it really had fallen by accident.

He could not see any marks, but a thought was forming at the back of his mind. He had seen the hammer and chisel, and immediately thought them ideal tools for smashing free a section of the wall.

They were also, he now realised with a warm glow of satisfaction and relief, exactly the tools to get him through the door. He ran back along the gully and collected them from the bucket.

The hammer was incredibly heavy and the

metal of the chisel was so cold he was afraid it would freeze to his hand. But Arthur managed to slide the thin end of the chisel into the gap between the door and its frame. He lined it up on the top bolt, jammed it hard in place and held it tight. Then he swung the hammer as hard as he dared.

His whole hand and wrist seemed to shudder under the impact. The door did not move. He tried again, swinging even harder and hoping he didn't miss and hit his hand. The hammer slammed into the splayed metal end of the chisel with a dull ringing round. The door shuddered as well this time and he felt it give. There was a metallic clatter from inside, but when he yanked out the chisel and peered through the gap he could still see the bolt.

Pulling hard at the door confirmed that the bolt was no longer doing its job. The sound must have been a screw coming free and falling down the stairs. The top of the door pulled towards Arthur, but the bottom remained firmly in position. So he repeated the process with the hammer and chisel on the bottom bolt.

Two more numbing blows with the hammer and the second bolt gave way as well, forced out of place by the chisel. Arthur returned hammer and chisel to the bucket and ripped the door open. Closing it behind him, he managed to push the disengaged screws back into place enough for the bolts to be held in position. At least it would look as if the door was secured now – until someone came to move the bolts.

But Arthur had no time to make a better job of it. He was shivering with the cold, afraid of being caught – though he argued with himself that he had done nothing wrong – and desperately hungry. The smell of bacon was wafting up from downstairs and, as soon as he was sure that the bolts would not just slip away as soon as he left them, Arthur went to find breakfast.

Dad was waiting for him outside the dining room. He seemed relieved to see Arthur.

'There you are. I was looking for you.'

'I woke up early,' Arthur said. 'I was just looking around. Sorry.'

But Dad did not seem to be annoyed, merely concerned. Arthur made to go into the dining room, but Dad was not following.

'Aren't we having breakfast?' Arthur asked.

'I've had mine. Well, coffee and toast.'

Something in Dad's tone told Arthur that there was more to his concern than just Arthur being late for breakfast. 'What is it?'

'I've had a message.' Dad forced a smile. 'You go and have breakfast, but I need to get back to London.'

'What? Why?'

'Something's come up apparently. It was all a bit garbled, but they need me back at the Yard this morning. Soon as possible.'

Arthur nodded. 'I'll grab a piece of toast and we can get going.'

But Dad was shaking his head. 'No, no. You stay here. I shan't be long. Back for lunch, I hope.' He smiled again, this time more genuinely. 'And I know how much you enjoy waiting round at work for me.'

It was true that Arthur found it boring sitting in someone else's office while Dad took longer than he had promised, talking to other people. But it was miles better than hanging around at Montgrave House.

'But, Dad—'

'I promise I won't be any longer than necessary,' Dad insisted. 'I'll give you a ring if I get delayed, but I expect it's nothing. Just some paperwork that needs signing off or they can't find where the coffee's kept. The usual crisis, you know.'

Arthur sighed. 'I know.' He nodded glumly. 'See you soon, then, Dad.'

Dad clapped him on the shoulder. 'That's the spirit.'

Arthur waved him goodbye, watching the car leave compressed tracks in the deepening snow as it set off down the driveway. Then he went back inside to have breakfast. The bacon would probably be burned to a crisp, he thought. It was.

The snow continued to fall throughout the morning. It was too cold to go outside, so Arthur sat in the drawing room in front of a large log fire and read his book. He was beginning to wish he'd brought his homework with him rather than promising himself he would rush through it on Sunday night when they got back home. To say that it was boring here was an understatement.

When he had read for what seemed like for ever although his watch insisted was only an hour, he got up and wandered round the room. It was littered with bric-à-brac and odds and ends. There were several occasional tables and even more cabinets and cupboards. Each and every surface seemed to be taken up with faded photographs, antique snuff boxes, empty vases. There was even a wooden tantalus – a sort of open box in which two heavy cut-glass sherry decanters were locked so that you needed a key to get a drink. Except that both decanters were empty.

Along almost the whole length of the outside wall was a window. It was criss-crossed with strips of lead, splitting the glass into diamonds that let in precious little light. Arthur stood for a while looking out at the segmented world beyond, watching the snow falling ever more rapidly. He could barely make out the small wooded area now and he despaired of Dad ever managing to get back for lunch.

But even as he thought he might be stuck here alone for the whole day, Arthur saw his dad. In the distance, obscured by the swirling snow, he could see him struggling back towards the house. He must have left the car on the main road – that would be gritted and clear, whereas the drive was now deep in snow. His hand raised in front of his face to ward off the snow and the wind, Dad battled his way towards the front door. Arthur ran from the room to meet him.

Mr Huntingdon was talking to the manager, Peters, in the hallway. They both turned abruptly as Arthur ran into view.

'I saw him – out there in the snow,' Arthur said breathlessly.

'In the snow?' Peters plainly had no idea what he was talking about.

But at that moment, the front door crashed open to admit a bedraggled, snow-covered figure.

'Good gracious,' Mr Huntingdon gasped. 'Are you all right?'

Arthur took a step forwards. Then he stopped. The man was wiping the snow from his face, his teeth were chattering and he was trying to speak. But this wasn't his dad. It was a complete stranger.

'Ashe,' he managed to stammer. 'Paul Ashe. My car – stuck out there in the snow. Slid off the road.'

'You'd better come and sit down,' Peters fussed. 'Let me get you a hot drink.'

He led the man towards the drawing room, with Huntingdon and Arthur following the wet trail left on the floor.

'We do excellent tea here at the Montgrave House Hotel,' Peters was saying.

'I tried to call the breakdown people,' Ashe

said, slumping in an uncomfortable leather armchair. 'Couldn't get a signal.'

'Ah, you won't. Not here,' Huntingdon told him. 'An important thing to consider really, when taking a holiday I mean. Mobile blind spots.' It was his next words that sent Arthur into despondency. 'And the phone lines are down too, I gather. No phones at all. We're completely cut off.'

Arthur could recall Huntingdon's exact words. There was no way he could have misunderstood or been mistaken. So when, half an hour later, a note was pushed under the door of his room, he stared at it in disbelief.

Had the phones been repaired? Or was Huntingdon wrong? Arthur had gone back to his room so that he could read in peace and would not have to listen to Mr Ashe any more. The man hadn't stopped talking – about how he was on his way to an important meeting and how there must surely be some means of helping him keep his appointment and how if only he had steered into the skid and how they should grit the roads round here properly ...

The note was handwritten in anonymous

block capitals on a piece of paper headed with the hotel's name and a crude line drawing of the house. It could have been taken from the pad in Arthur's own room. It said:

YOUR FATHER RANG. THE SNOW IS SO BAD HE CAN'T GET BACK TODAY. HE IS STUCK IN LONDON BUT WILL SEE YOU TOMORROW.

It was not signed. There was no clue as to who might have taken the message or when it had been written. Or how Dad had managed to ring when the phones were not working.

Almost sixty miles away, in an office in New Scotland Yard, Arthur's dad had received a message of his own. Having driven for nearly two hours through the snow, he had been less than amused to discover that nobody at the Yard seemed to know who had left the message telling him to return. The more he asked and probed, the less he believed that he was needed at all.

And now he had another message. Detective Constable Jenkins was apologetic. 'It was a terrible line. Like someone was frying chips next to the phone.'

'But he definitely said not to go back?'

'Oh, yes.' Jenkins was sure about that. 'Said he was your boy Arthur and could I let you know that the snow's so bad they've closed all the roads for miles around. Not to try to get back to him till tomorrow.' Jenkins shrugged. 'He said he'd be all right and not to worry.'

'Nothing else to do, I suppose,' Arthur's dad admitted. 'Just wait for the weather to clear.'

'I guess so, sir. Funny we've not had reports of the roads being impassable down that way.' He stepped back out of the office, pausing to observe, 'Still, you know what it's like. They're probably so impassable no one's got through with that news. A bit of snow and the country grinds to a dead halt.'

Arthur's dad nodded. It couldn't be helped, and at least Arthur was somewhere safe. 'Well, son,' he muttered, 'it looks like you're on your own for now.'

Chapter 6

Jonny stood watching the entrance to Scotland Yard for several minutes after Inspector Gilbertson had gone inside. What was happening? Gilbertson had come to the Invisible Detective before for help, so why did he now conceal his identity when asking questions? Why not wait until everyone else had left and be plain about his request? Or was there something more to it than this?

He was still pondering these questions when a sudden movement caught his attention. He had been half watching the people going in and coming out of Scotland Yard. Some were uniformed police, others were in plain clothes – either police or members of the public. But all were moving at a calm and mannered pace, as if awed by the building itself. What caught Jonny's attention was a blur of motion as someone came running out with no attempt to conceal their anger and complete lack of respect.

It was a young woman. She was, Jonny guessed, in her twenties. She was wearing a long, elegant coat against the cold and she was shaking with anger and emotion. She stopped under the light outside the building, close to where Jonny was, and dabbed at her eyes with a handkerchief she pulled from her coat sleeve.

The woman saw Jonny as she pushed the handkerchief away. She took a few steps towards him and he shrank back. He wondered if he should just turn and run off, but that would be even more rude than watching her crying.

'What are you looking at, young man?' she demanded.

'I'm sorry,' Jonny said quickly. 'I was just . . . Well, you looked upset. I wondered if I could help.'

Her face seemed to melt into a smile at this. She walked the last few steps over to where Jonny was standing and reached out a gloved hand to touch his cheek. 'How very kind and considerate,' she said quietly. 'So much more polite and civilised than those barbarians in there.' She sniffed and nodded back at the entrance to Scotland Yard.

Jonny was not sure what to do now. He could not just leave, yet he didn't really know what to say. 'Are you all right, miss?' he asked. It seemed rather silly and inadequate. But it made her smile sadly again.

The woman took a deep breath. 'I am fine,' she announced. 'I came here to ask for help, but it seems that there is nothing wrong and I am being ridiculous.' She paused to pull out the hanky and dab at her eyes again. 'Oh dear, how silly you must think me. I am so sorry.'

She started walking towards the Victoria Embankment and Jonny walked with her, uncertain what to do.

'My brother,' she said at last, her voice sounding stronger and more determined, 'has disappeared.'

'And you came to the police for help finding him?'

She nodded. 'But they do not seem overly concerned. They say he won't come to any harm, that he is a grown man and can look after himself and will return when he is ready.' She sighed heavily. 'They don't realise how weak and frail he is. My brother,' she went on, turning to fix Jonny with a sad but intense look, 'is not a well man.'

'I'm sorry.'

'Oh, he was always sickly as a child. But with

my help and support he had made such progress. Now, I fear . . .' Her voice tailed off and they walked in silence for a while.

'Can I help?' Jonny asked as they turned on to the Embankment.

'You?'

Jonny was about to suggest she come back to the consulting session, but it would probably be over by now. He didn't think she would want to wait a whole week for an offer of help. 'I could look for your brother. If he is lost around here. I mean, I know the area. I have friends who can help.'

She stopped and shook her head. 'So very kind,' she murmured. 'And you don't even know my name.'

'You could tell me,' Jonny pointed out.

She laughed at that, a high-pitched, tinkling sound that brought her face to life and made Jonny smile with delight. She held out her hand. 'Miss Waters,' she said, and Jonny shook her hand. 'Miss Vera Waters.'

'Jonny Levin,' Jonny said.

'And my brother is Edwin Waters. The last I heard of him, he had lodgings in Blackfriars. I found out that much, but then the trail ended and I have been unable to trace his movements after he left his lodgings there.' She stared off into the distance. 'But originally we are from Cricklewood, of course.'

'Cricklewood?' Jonny was startled by the name. Immediately he was embarrassed by his reaction, seeing that Miss Waters was looking at him in surprise. 'I'm sorry. I was just thinking, well . . .' He laughed. 'Perhaps the Hunchback of Cricklewood got him.'

It was not a good thing to say. Miss Waters's demeanour changed immediately. Her nostrils flared and her face was drained of colour. 'Don't be stupid,' she hissed.

'I'm sorry.' He was surprised at the vehemence of her reaction.

'The Hunchback of Cricklewood!'

Jonny took a step back from her. 'Sorry,' he repeated. 'Just a daft thing to say.'

But she was not listening. 'Of course the hunchback got him,' she said. 'If I don't find Edwin soon,' she said loudly and angrily and entirely seriously, 'then the hunchback will kill him.'

* * *

Jonny left Miss Waters at the Embankment. She seemed calmer and headed off towards the tube. Jonny made his way back to Cannon Street and was in time to see the first people coming out from the Invisible Detective's consulting session. He had expected it to be over – there must have been a few last-minute questions, or maybe some comment on the mysterious stranger that Jonny now knew was Inspector Gilbertson.

Rather than push his way through the people who were emerging, Jonny decided to wait for Art and Meg outside. He thought about going back to the den to see Flinch – she didn't always attend the Invisible Detective's sessions, finding them a bit boring. But instead, he watched the people making their way over to the fair. The coconut shy was still set up on the corner and there was a tent advertising a bearded lady, which he and Art had found especially disappointing when they sneaked a look through the door the previous week. 'It's a man in a dress,' Art had whispered, and Jonny could not disagree.

As he stood there, Jonny became aware that other people were watching too. It slowly dawned on him that he was not the only person sneaking furtive glances at the locksmith's shop. Several men were also watching, exchanging subtle looks and waves. All of them were wearing similar raincoats and hats. As if to reinforce the point, one man wandered – far too casually – up to another and the two spoke briefly and checked their watches. Then they parted company and continued staring at the door. It was not a huge leap of imagination for Jonny to work out that the watchers were plain-clothes policemen. But why were they there?

The last few people were leaving the session. Jonny saw – and heard – Albert Norris crossing the street and making his way back towards the Dog and Goose.

He remembered how Art had told them that his dad said the police had a suspect for the attacks – someone who was an expert at disappearing. Jonny suddenly felt weak at the knees as he realised who that suspect must be. The police were there watching and waiting for Brandon Lake – for the Invisible Detective. And at any moment now the Invisible Detective, in the form of Meg and Art, would walk out of the locksmith's and straight into a trap.

The bedroom was cold and draughty, and being in it only reminded Arthur that he was all on his own. He did not want to speak to anyone, but being downstairs, where he could at least hear the sounds of other people, might make the loneliness and boredom more bearable.

Actually, he reflected, the library was quite interesting, in a dusty, old-fashioned sort of way. There were wooden bookshelves from floor to ceiling on most of the wall space. In the middle of the room was a reading table with a couple of dilapidated upright chairs beside it. The seats were faded and the padding so thin as to be non-existent. Yesterday's newspaper was open on the table and Arthur spent a few minutes leafing through it. But there was nothing very interesting inside.

He turned his attention to the books. All of them seemed to be old. Arthur guessed there was nothing less than fifty years old in the entire room apart from himself and the newspaper. The nearest shelves were all biology textbooks of some sort –

bound journals of various societies, ancient copies of the medical journal the *Lancet* and a history of ancient Greece that seemed to have got there by accident.

Disappointed, Arthur moved towards the next set of shelves. There was a long, narrow window in between and he paused as he went past, glancing at the swirling snow outside and wondering if Dad was ever going to be able to get back. Perhaps he would be stuck here into next week. Great.

A movement at the edge of the window startled Arthur. It took him a moment to realise what it was, and by the time he had, it had gone.

It was a face. Someone had been looking in. Probably there was a perfectly reasonable explanation for that – but why had whoever it was quickly ducked out of sight when they saw Arthur looking at them? He waited a full minute, peering out into the snow and trying to see round and below the window. But there was no sign of anyone now.

'Oh, sorry.'

The voice made him turn sharply.

Mrs Smith was hesitating in the doorway. 'I was looking for the paper,' she said, slightly nervous as ever.

Arthur wondered what she was so anxious about – she seemed to be constantly on edge. 'That's OK,' he said. 'It's on the table, but it's yesterday's, I'm afraid.'

'Oh.' She seemed not to mind and sat at the table, pulling the paper towards her and studying the front-page headlines.

'Probably couldn't get today's because of the snow,' Arthur said. It was nice just to talk to someone, he realised.

But Mrs Smith seemed not to be of the same opinion. She glanced up, smiled for a split second, then returned to the paper. Arthur watched her for a moment, then he went to see what was on the next bookshelf.

It seemed to be chemistry books. Was the whole library given over to old science books and papers, Arthur wondered? He turned to make a comment to Mrs Smith, trying again to start a conversation. But she had gone, the paper left open on the table.

The next shelf along was taken up with an ancient edition of the *Encyclopaedia Britannica*. It was so old that the gold lettering on the spine had flaked off and some of the leather binding was pulling away. There was a click from behind Arthur, the sound of the door closing. Caught in a draught perhaps, he thought idly as he ran his finger along the books, leaving a trail in the dust. There was a crackling sound too. Like the crumpling up of paper. Someone else must have come in.

But the room was empty. And the door was, as Arthur had expected, closed. What he had not expected was that the newspaper on the table was now crunched into balls that were on fire.

The room was quickly filling with smoke as the fire spread from one scrunched-up page to the next, leaping to the carpet and immediately catching. The air was hot and dusty, making Arthur cough and splutter. Gasping for breath, he ran for the door.

It was locked.

The room was full of smoke now. The fire had spread to one of the bookshelves and the spines of the books were curling in the heat. One peeled free and caught light like a taper. Soon the flames would eat into the body of the book.

Arthur slammed his fist into the door. His mouth was too choked with the acrid smoke to shout for help. He hammered on the wood, his eyes smarting and tears produced by frustration, fear and smoke rolling down his cheeks. Slowly, he collapsed against the door, sliding down and lying on the floor.

There was less smoke low down and Arthur was able to gulp in air. The window, he thought – he could smash the window and get out that way. But he seemed to be unable to stand. His legs had turned to jelly – as if the bones had already melted in the rising heat. He tried to crawl, but after only a short distance he slumped to the floor again. He rolled on to his back, his head swimming and his vision blurred.

It was at that point that a whole panel of the door suddenly exploded inwards. The wood splintered and shattered and a large boot came into view through the swirling smoke. Just for a second, then it was gone. Arthur tried to lever himself up on his elbow. Another large piece of wood flew from the door and rolled across the room. Someone was forcing their way in – a tall dark figure carrying something.

Arthur saw with surprise that it was the groundsman, Bill. What he was holding was a garden hose and within seconds of entering the room a jet of water was splashing off the table and dousing the flames. The smoke started to clear immediately.

Despite the heat and the smoke, it was just the newspaper and the books on one of the shelves that seemed to be burning. Arthur managed to crawl towards the door. Bill looked down at him as he made his way slowly past. For a moment, Arthur was reminded of the face he had glimpsed at the window – had it been Bill, watching him for some reason? Was that how he knew that the fire had started? Or had he actually started the fire? If so, surely he would not then rush in to put it out. Nothing made any sense at the moment. Arthur pushed his way through the shattered remains of the door and slumped into a chair in the hallway outside.

Mrs Smith was standing there with Mr Huntingdon. Neither of them seemed to notice Arthur. Huntingdon was trying to soothe the young woman, who was in floods of tears.

'I could have been killed,' she wailed. 'I was in there just now. Oh, this is awful.'

Don't mind me, Arthur thought. He rubbed at his eyes, which were stinging and sore.

'And of course we can't dial 999 because the phones are down,' Huntingdon was saying.

Mr Smith arrived to take control of his wife,

putting his arm round her and leading her away. Arthur watched them go. First the stone almost falling on him, then the fire in the library. It occurred to him that Mr Smith had been with him for the first of these, Mrs Smith for the second. It was easy to assume that if they weren't accidents, then someone meant to harm Arthur. But perhaps it was the Smiths who were the real targets.

Or perhaps he was imagining it. The stone could have fallen on its own. And the fire . . . Well, maybe there was a faulty connection in the wiring in there. Everything else seemed to be old and worn out, so why not the electrical wiring too?

Mr Huntingdon was offering advice to Bill through the door. It sounded as if the fire was almost out and, to listen to him, you would think that was all due to Mr Huntingdon. Cold outside or not, Arthur needed some fresh air. His clothes stank of smoke and he seemed to have bitter flecks from the burnt paper stuck in his mouth.

It was still snowing and it was bitterly cold, but right now Arthur welcomed that. He walked for what seemed like hours, his tracks disappearing again in the snow.

Eventually he wondered if there was a message from Dad – if the phones had been fixed. Or if Dad had returned. He trudged back towards the hotel, kicking at the deep snow and sending it up in miniature blizzards in front of him.

Arthur was approaching the house from the side. He did not think he had seen it from this angle before. There was a yard enclosed by a wall, a wide entranceway opening to the side of the house. He paused to glance in. In one corner of the yard, close to the hotel wall, was what looked like a huge snowdrift. Something had been buried.

Because he wanted to occupy his mind – to take it off thoughts of fire and falling masonry as much as anything – Arthur walked over to examine the mound of snow. As he approached, he could see that there was a definite shape beneath the white blanket. It was a car.

Even before he scraped away the snow from the end of the mound, Arthur had a horrible notion that he already knew what he would find. As the snow fell away to reveal the dark paintwork beneath, as the boot and back of the large black car were exposed, his worst suspicions confirmed.

He stood back, looking through the tumbling snow at the rear of the car. The effect was like looking through mist or smoke. Or exhaust fumes. And Arthur knew that he had seen this car before – speeding away after almost hitting him. It was the car that the man with the beard had tried to force him into outside school.

There was no longer any doubt. Someone at Montgrave House – though he didn't know who or why – intended something very nasty to happen to Arthur Drake.

Chapter 7

Jonny pushed past the last few people on the stairs. A couple of them looked at him irritably as they moved aside to let him up, but most paid little attention. They were laughing and joking and chattering as usual.

The room was empty when he reached the top of the stairs. The curtain twitched, then it was tugged aside. Meg had heard Jonny's urgent footsteps on the way up. She stood there looking at him, hands on hips, as if to say, 'And where have you been?'

But Jonny ignored her. 'Art,' he called. 'Art, quick – it's the police. They think Brandon Lake is the hunchback.'

'What?' Art was out of the chair in a moment and slipping off the heavy coat. 'What do you mean?'

'I followed that man. It was Inspector Gilbertson. When I got back, there were plain-clothes police outside, watching.' He looked from Art to Meg and back again. 'You said your dad thought the police suspect was an expert at disappearing. Like the Invisible Detective.'

Meg seemed less concerned than Jonny. 'So what?'

'So they're waiting for Brandon Lake to leave. And if he doesn't, they'll come in here to find him,' Jonny said.

Art said nothing. His face was lined with thought and he paced slowly up and down.

'But they'll just find us,' Meg pointed out. 'Brandon Lake isn't here.'

'No,' Art agreed. 'But they'll wonder where he went. They'll ask the last people to leave – they'll have noted who they were. They'll question them and discover that Brandon Lake was still here. They'll think about that and pretty soon they'll work it all out.'

'You mean,' Meg said, 'they'll know the truth about the Invisible Detective?'

Art nodded glumly. 'And at the moment only us three and Flinch know that. It won't be possible to keep it secret once the police know. Word will soon spread.'

'That's if they don't lock us up for the attacks,' Jonny pointed out. 'What are we going to do?'

'We can't just leave or they'll guess it's us

anyway,' Art said. 'And if we simply stay here, they'll eventually come in and . . .' He stopped and held up his hand to tell the others to keep quiet.

Someone was coming up the stairs. They could all hear the unmistakable sound of feet heading quickly towards the room.

'Too late,' Meg said.

But Art broke into a grin. 'I don't think so.' The feet were quickening their pace, running up the stairs now. Not the heavy-booted feet of a policeman but the lighter, swifter sound of a child. Art raised his voice: 'Hello, Flinch,' he called.

'You were a long time today. I got bored,' Flinch said as she came into the room, out of breath. 'I wanted to go to the fair again. But . . .' She ran over to where Art was standing. 'There are men outside, watching. I think they're going to come in here in a minute.'

'We know,' Meg said. 'It's a problem.'

Detective Constable Davies had gathered the others together. There were four of them in total. They had watched everyone leaving the session. Gilbertson had made it clear he did not want Brandon Lake brought in for questioning while there were other people there. Partly it would not be fair on the so-called Invisible Detective, but more importantly there might be an outcry – the man could escape in the confusion.

Gilbertson himself had attended the Invisible Detective's session in a last attempt to convince himself that Brandon Lake was not a viable suspect. When he emerged, he had nodded to Davies – the slightest inclination of the head, just enough to give the order: 'Bring him in.'

Now Davies was ready to do just that. He had hoped that Brandon Lake would follow his audience out of the locksmith's shop soon after they all left. But it seemed that he was staying put. Davies knew there was no other exit. The only window gave out on to Cannon Street as well, so there really was no escape for the man.

'Right, lads,' Davies said.

But one of the others interrupted. 'Look, here he comes.'

He was right. A figure was emerging cautiously, almost surreptitiously, from the locksmith's. A tall, thin man dressed in a long overcoat stepped out into the street. For a moment he stood in the light of a nearby streetlamp.

Davies caught a brief glimpse of him – a scarf wrapped tight round his face, perhaps against the cold or perhaps to hide his features. His hat was pulled down low over the eyes. Brandon Lake.

Davies felt a thrill of excitement. He had seen the Invisible Detective – perhaps he and his colleagues were the first people ever to see him, ever to see him and know who he was anyway. The tall man looked round, as if to check he was not being watched, then, without apparently noticing Davies and the others, started down the street.

The Invisible Detective walked quickly but seemed a little unsteady on his feet. He looked to be struggling to keep his head still – perhaps afraid that his scarf would slip or that his hat would fall off and reveal the man beneath.

'Let's get him,' Davies said, and set off in pursuit.

Almost immediately, it seemed that Brandon Lake had spotted them. He broke into a hesitant run and Davies quickened his pace.

They were almost at the Dog and Goose and Davies was afraid his quarry might go into the pub. He could lose himself in the mass of people inside – after all, they had only his coat, hat and scarf by which to recognise him. But luckily Brandon Lake kept going, turning instead into the narrow alleyway behind the pub.

'We've got him now,' one of the men said. 'That's a dead end. Goes nowhere.'

'Yes,' Davies agreed, pausing for breath at the end of the alley. 'I reckon the Invisible Detective has just made his greatest mistake.' He took out his torch and the others did the same. 'Come on.'

With a feeling of satisfaction and excitement, Davies stepped into the alleyway. It was not wide and it ran only the length of the pub before ending in a high brick wall. There were empty barrels stacked up against the side wall, but they would have heard if anyone had tried to clamber up them. In any case, the wall was the back of a warehouse – there was nowhere to climb to.

Also, Davies was sure there had not been time for anyone to get to the back door of the pub, which was locked when he tried it.

Yet the alleyway was empty. The Invisible Detective had vanished. There were just a couple of kids rummaging through the dustbins and behind the barrels.

'Lost our ball,' one of them said guiltily. 'It bounced in here, now we can't find it. You lost or something?'

'Where did he go?' Davies demanded.

'Who?'

'The man who just came down here.' The boy looked at him blankly. The other, younger kid was coming over now – curious. 'You must have seen him,' Davies insisted.

'We ain't seen no one, mister,' the younger kid said. 'No one's been in this alley except us.'

The others were looking to Davies for instructions. While he was speaking to the children they had walked the length of the alley, shining their torches into every conceivable hiding place. One of the men shook his head – nothing.

Davies sighed in frustration. He was the one who would have to break the news to Inspector Gilbertson. The news that the Invisible Detective had more than lived up to his reputation and had vanished into thin air.

140

Whereas dinner the previous night had been punctuated by non-stop claims from Mr Smith that he might have been killed, Saturday night's meal was interspersed with his claims that his wife might have been killed. He made it clear several times that, were it not for the snow, they would be leaving.

Mr Peters was suitably apologetic. Mr Huntingdon nodded as if he agreed with them both. Mrs Trefusis was as brusque as before and treated the matter as if it had not happened. Everyone ignored Arthur. The only change so far as he could see was that Miss Napier, the nurse-cum-waitress, seemed to be watching her employer through narrowed eyes. She said nothing the whole time she waited at the table, but Arthur got the impression that tonight more than ever she resented Mrs Trefusis's abrupt manner.

Arthur went straight to his room after dinner. He closed the heavy wooden door and locked it. It was an old mortise lock, but it seemed strong enough and the door was certainly sturdy. He took the key out of the lock and put it on the bedside cabinet. After a moment's thought, he then jammed the upright chair that stood in the corner of the room under the door handle.

There was a small balcony outside the window, with a glass door opening on to it. Arthur went and stood in the cold of the night for several minutes, gathering his thoughts. But really, he decided, he did not know what to think. The sooner Dad got back and they could leave, the better. He was shivering from fear as much as the cold.

He went back inside and closed the door to the balcony. There was a bolt at the bottom. It didn't look very strong, but Arthur shot it home anyway. Then he lay on his bed and read. He gave up almost immediately. His eyes refused to focus on the page and his mind refused to focus on the story. He put the book down and looked over at the empty bed beside his own – Dad's bed.

What might have been hours or only minutes later, Arthur got undressed, pulled on his pyjamas, washed, brushed his teeth and got into bed. He turned the light off, but left the curtains open. There was a moon and the room seemed to glow slightly in the pale light reflected off the snow outside. It was eerie but at the same time comforting.

He felt as if he had not slept at all. But it was darker now and, when he angled it to catch the light,

Arthur's watch told him it was gone two in the morning. At the edge of his consciousness there was a sound.

It came again. A sort of rattle. He closed his eyes, drifting off once more, vaguely wondering what the noise could be – traffic on the main road perhaps. But no, Arthur thought, it was the middle of the night, and anyway the roads were blocked with snow. He was wide awake now, sitting up suddenly as he became aware of what the noise really sounded like.

Someone was trying to open the door. In the moonlight he could see the handle moving. He imagined he could see the door rattling in its frame as someone tried to push it open. Whoever it was became increasingly frustrated and determined, the rattle of wood on wood reaching a machine-gun ferocity. Arthur shrank back into the bed, wanting to pull the covers over his head but knowing that would not make things any better.

Then the noise stopped. There was another sound now. Distant, rhythmic, insistent. It was the ringing of a telephone. Arthur got nervously out of bed and went over to the door. He tried to see through the keyhole, to make out who could be trying to get into the room. Should he call out? If it was Dad, surely he would say something to Arthur.

A dark shape moved on the other side of the door. Then there was more light behind the keyhole as whoever it was stepped quickly away. He could hear the thump of their feet on the floor, beating time to the ringing of the phone. Distant now, going downstairs. The ringing stopped. Had the caller given up? Or had the person at the door answered the phone?

Arthur strained to hear. He was half tempted to open the door, but he was too afraid. People didn't usually ring up in the middle of the night unless it was an emergency of some sort. Was it Dad?

He could just make out a voice. Someone shouting. Indistinct. Coming to a decision, Arthur moved the chair, grabbed the key from the bedside cabinet and opened the door. He ran on tiptoes to the top of the stairs and leaned over the banister, trying to hear the voice from below.

It was clearer now, but Arthur heard only one short phrase. Then there was the clatter of the phone being slammed down and the footsteps started back towards the stairs, getting louder and closer.

Quick as he could, Arthur ran back to his room and shut the door. It was a temptation to slam it, but he did not want whoever it was to know for certain he was in the room. He had caught only a few words and he had not recognised the husky, angry voice that had shouted them into the phone.

'Because he's as good as dead, that's why.'

He locked the door and jammed the chair back in place before sitting on the edge of the bed, fixated on the door handle, hoping and praying it would not move again.

But it did.

A sudden violent movement threatened to wrench the handle right off. It was accompanied by a loud thump as something hit the other side of the door. Arthur imagined he could see the wooden panelling bulge under the blow – if it *was* imagination.

Another thump. And another. This continued for what seemed like hours and Arthur was convinced that in a minute the door would collapse. He was looking desperately round the room for somewhere to hide. Under one of the beds? Too obvious. Behind the door? Dangerous – he might get hurt when it finally crashed open. The bathroom? The door to the small en-suite was not going to hold out if the heavy main door to the room gave way.

The balcony? That seemed like the only place. He could not hope to hide out there for long. It was probably the first place anyone would look. Unless he could climb down to ground level. His room was on the first floor, so there was only one storey below. Was there a drainpipe running down to the ground? Could he climb down that and hide in the grounds?

The door to the balcony refused to open. Arthur heaved on it, felt it give – then remembered the bolt. He had almost torn the socket away from the frame. But as he fumbled with the bolt, the hammering on the main door stopped.

He froze. Listened. Strained to hear. There was movement outside the door, shuffling, murmuring, whispering. Then footsteps.

Arthur waited by the balcony door for several minutes before he dared return to the main door. He removed the chair as quietly as he could and peered through the keyhole. The corridor outside looked to be empty. But was it?

He stood hesitating by the door, wondering if he dared open it and see. How quickly could he slam the door again if someone was out there waiting? Now that it seemed the phones were working again, he was desperate to get downstairs and call Dad — let him know what was happening here. Surely the police could find a way through? This was an emergency.

The voice was barely more than a whisper, but it made Arthur jump back from the door, clutching his chest as his head hammered almost as loud as the whisper.

'Are you there?'

Should he answer? Who was it?

'Arthur Drake — are you all right?'

It was a woman's voice. Miss Napier, he was sure. Relieved, Arthur reached for the key. Then he stopped. What if it was Miss Napier who had been trying to get in?

'Are you awake?' the voice hissed.

Or what if it wasn't Miss Napier at all? What if he was wrong? Arthur collapsed to the floor, sitting with his back to the door.

'I just wanted to check you're OK,' the voice hissed. 'I heard noises from up here.'

Arthur said nothing. After another minute there was an audible sigh from outside, then footsteps moving away down the corridor.

By four o'clock, Arthur could wait no longer. He unlocked the door, cursing at the way the key scraped noisily in the lock. The corridor was empty. Closing the door quietly behind him, he ran as fast as he could to the stairs and down into the entrance hallway below.

He remembered that there was a telephone on the reception table. It had a coin box built in and, according to the instructions on a faded label glued to the top, you pushed your coins in when someone at the other end answered.

Arthur had no coins. All his loose change was in his trouser pocket upstairs in his room. He thought about going back, but decided against it. If he called Dad, then surely he would guess it was Arthur and call back. Or if he didn't, then Arthur could get the coins. Or he could dial 999 – emergency calls were apparently free of charge.

He lifted the handset, his fingers tapping out his home number. But there was something wrong,

Arthur realised, as he put the handset to his ear. He could hear nothing – not even the dial tone.

The phone was completely dead.

Chapter 8

It was Tuesday night and the Cannoniers were all gathered at the den. The main topic of conversation, apart from Brandon Lake's inspired escape from the police, was what they should do about next week's session. Meg was in favour of cancelling it, but none of the others were ready yet to agree to that.

'We can't just wait for the police to turn up again to arrest Brandon Lake,' Meg pointed out. 'We could leave a notice on the door. Due to unforeseen circumstances . . .' It seemed straightforward enough.

'Unforeseen?' Jonny laughed, but not with humour. 'He's a detective. He's supposed to know stuff.'

'But that isn't the real problem anyway,' Art said. 'We need to clear the Invisible Detective's name somehow.'

'How?' Meg demanded.

'I don't know,' he admitted.

'But Brandon Lake can't clear his name if he's in hiding,' Jonny said. 'And how long before he loses his reputation and people just don't turn up any more, whether he's there or not?'

'Why don't we tell Art's dad?' Flinch asked.

'Tell him what?' Meg asked.

Flinch shrugged. 'Everything. He'd understand.'

Actually, Meg thought, he probably would. Though how he would react when he discovered that Brandon Lake did not exist and it was his own son and his friends who were the Invisible Detective, she didn't know.

'There is someone else we could ask to help,' Art said.

'Oh?' Meg wondered who.

'You're forgetting,' he told her. 'It's Tuesday today.'

Then she realised. 'Of course. Charlie.'

Flinch grinned and Jonny laughed. It seemed the obvious solution now that Art mentioned it.

'Did someone call my name?'

The voice came from the back of the dusty warehouse. A figure was walking slowly towards them, picking his way through the rolls of disintegrating carpet. Charlie – Lord Fotherington – was an elderly man with an amazing shock of white hair. His hat was jammed down on top of it, struggling to keep it under control. He was wearing a dark overcoat and carrying a silver-topped cane. As usual, he smiled at the children like a favourite uncle. He flicked the tails of his coat over the back of a roll of carpet as he sat down.

On Tuesdays, when he was free, Charlie treated the Cannoniers to tea at the station café. The children had helped Charlie on several occasions and they had shared some dangerous adventures together. With the worry of the police and everything, Meg had quite forgotten that Charlie might come – as, it seemed, had Jonny and Flinch. Maybe Art had forgotten too, she thought, or maybe he had seen Charlie come in.

'Hello, Charlie,' Art said. He came straight to the point. 'I wonder if you can help us,' he said. 'We have a bit of a problem, you see. Or rather, Brandon Lake has a bit of a problem.'

So far as Charlie knew, the Invisible Detective did exist and the Cannoniers – Art, Meg, Jonny and Flinch – helped him out. Like the Baker Street Irregulars in the Sherlock Holmes stories, Art said. But Meg had never read any, so she was none the wiser.

Charlie held his hand up to stop Art. 'Would this problem,' he said slowly and deliberately, 'be anything to do with the fact that several plain-clothes police officers tried to attract his attention last night, but lost him somewhere behind the Dog and Goose?'

'Have you come here to arrest us?' Flinch asked seriously.

Meg stifled a smile.

Charlie gave a short laugh. 'No, Miss Flinch. I may on occasion be asked for my advice by the police, or even, as you know, the Prime Minister, but I don't arrest people. In fact, I came here to buy you tea as usual. But I do have a message that I would be grateful if you could pass on to Mr Lake for me. Or rather, for Inspector Gilbertson of Scotland Yard.'

Art nodded. He looked worried. 'I take it they want him to give himself up.'

Charlie's eyebrows rose up at this. 'Indeed not. The message is more in the nature of an apology. And a plea for help.'

'What?' The children exchanged looks.

'You see, while Constable Davies and his colleagues were watching the Invisible

Detective's consulting session yesterday evening, the real culprit of these crimes was attacking a young man at the fair. Behind the Whack a Rat attraction – if attraction is the right word.' He beamed round at them. 'So the Invisible Detective is off the hook. He and the attacker may both be able to vanish into thin air, but nobody seriously believes that the Invisible Detective can be in two places at once.'

Meg was so relieved at the news that she was tempted to tell Charlie that actually the Invisible Detective could be in four places at once. But her relief did not last, as a less pleasant thought occurred to her.

'The man who was attacked – is he all right?'

Charlie's smile vanished and he nodded gravely. 'The doctors say he will make a full recovery. But he has lost a lot of blood. Another mystery there.'

'The blood?' Art said.

Flinch pulled a disgusted face.

'Lost, as I said. As in, unaccounted for. Where did it go?'

'Assuming Brandon Lake accepts the apology . . .' Art said.

'He will,' Flinch put in quickly.

'Then what is this plea for help you mentioned?'

'Yes,' Meg said. 'What does Inspector Gilbertson want?'

'Inspector Gilbertson would like the detective's help in mobilising the local people to keep watch and report any suspicious persons.' Charlie leaned forward, his chin resting on the silver tip of his cane. 'Hunchbacks in particular, of course. Though there is nothing innately wrong with being a hunchback and there are probably several employed by various sideshows at the fair. So it may be merely myth and exaggeration that attribute these attacks to a hunchback. But the police must leave no avenue unexplored.' He gave a short laugh. 'Which brings me to a small request of my own, actually.'

'Which is?' Art asked.

'Anything we can do,' Meg told him.

Jonny was nodding enthusiastically.

'Well, perhaps you could indulge my curiosity enough to explain how the inestimable Mr Lake managed his disappearing act last night. Constable Davies was by all accounts extremely mystified, not to say frustrated. Though I promise not to divulge any trade secrets.'

They all looked at Art.

'What do you think?' Jonny asked.

'Would Mr Lake mind if we demonstrated?' Meg wondered.

'Oh, let's,' Flinch implored.

Art smiled. 'I think we could make an exception to the strict secrecy rules in this case.' He turned to Flinch. 'Why don't you and I go and fetch Brandon Lake, and he can explain it himself.'

Charlie was startled at this suggestion. 'Good gracious, I was only asking about the disappearing act. I didn't expect an audience with the elusive detective himself.' He frowned. 'Er, will I have to be blindfolded or something?'

'No,' Meg told him. 'Nothing like that.'

Art and Flinch were making their way to the back of the warehouse. Jonny, Meg and Charlie watched them disappear from sight. Then they looked round at each other. Nobody spoke.

Jonny eventually said, 'Here he is.'

Meg and Charlie turned to look. A tall, thin man dressed in a long coat and wearing a hat was walking slightly awkwardly across the warehouse towards them. As he got closer, Meg could see that his scarf was over the lower part of his face so that only his eyes were visible under the brim of his hat. They were shining with amusement and delight, and Meg could not help but smile back.

'Brandon Lake?' There was something close to awe in Charlie's voice as he stood up and offered his hand.

'This,' said Meg, 'is how he disappears.'

Charlie leaned forwards, as if expecting the man to evaporate into the ether. But that did not happen. Instead, the coat fell to the floor, followed immediately by the hat and the scarf. They were kicked quickly out of sight. Charlie gave a laugh of astonishment and clapped his hands together.

Standing in front of him was Art, with Flinch sitting on his shoulders. Art bent down enough for her to jump off – and where there had moments before been a tall, thin man wearing a long coat, a hat and a scarf, there were now two laughing children.

On the short walk down to the station café, Art explained to Charlie how Brandon Lake had recognised Inspector Gilbertson's voice when he attended the Invisible Detective's consulting session.

'So when Art and Flinch distracted the police and led them away,' Meg concluded, 'Mr Lake just slipped out of the locksmith's and went home.'

Tea was lively and fun. All the children were in high spirits after Charlie's news that the Invisible Detective was no longer being sought by the police. Flinch, as usual, tucked into fruit cake. The others drank tea and helped out with the cake when they could get at it.

They were still laughing and joking when, after nearly an hour, Charlie looked across the café and said, 'I see we have a visitor.'

Art turned to see who had come in – and was greeted by the unexpected sight of his father, walking purposefully across the café towards them.

'I thought I might find you all in here,' Peter Drake said as he arrived at the table. There were chairs nearby but he made no attempt to draw one up and join them.

'Were you looking for me?' Art asked. 'Or Charlie?'

'All of you, I suppose.' His face was grave and his tone severe.

Art wondered what he had done wrong. But his father's next words dispelled any sense of guilt and made his blood run cold.

'There's been another attack,' Art's dad said. 'In the mirror maze at the Wilkinson Gallery. In broad daylight. And again the attacker just seemed to vanish. I came here straight away.'

'It's serious, isn't it?' Art said.

His father nodded. 'You could say that. A man is dead.'

At what time Arthur finally got back to sleep, he had no idea. He dozed fitfully, his dreams peppered with images of doors smashing down and Bill the groundsman's boot crashing through them. He saw black cars and bearded men, falling stonework and enormous drifts of snow.

And through it all he heard the scrape and scratch of someone trying to get into his room.

When he finally woke, the scratching-scraping

was still there, as if trapped behind his eyes. He focused on his watch – propped against the book on the bedside cabinet – and was astonished to see it was nearly nine o'clock. It might be Sunday, but he had not expected or intended to lie in.

The scraping and scratching became a tapping now – like a branch blowing against a window. A window. Arthur turned over quickly to check the balcony.

Outside, silhouetted against the white of the cloudy sky, was a dark figure. Its shape was impossible to discern as it was wrapped in a huge coat that was speckled with snow. The figure was short and hunched and was tapping on the glass of the door.

At the bottom of the door, Arthur could see the bolt was not going to hold. If the figure pushed at the door, it would open easily. He leaped out of bed and ran for the main door.

The window crashed open as the figure pushed its way into the room.

Arthur was at the door now, turning the handle. But the door refused to open – locked. The key was back by the bed. And the figure from outside was in the room now. It was straightening up, throwing back the hood of its coat, shaking its head to let a mass of dark hair cascade out. Arthur stared in utter disbelief.

'Sarah?' he said. 'What are you doing here?'

Sarah Bustle grinned at him. She turned to close the door behind her and then flopped down on the bed, undoing her coat. 'Saving your life, I expect,' she said. 'Goodness, it's cold out there. Why didn't you let me in, you twerp?'

Arthur sat down on the other bed, his heart still going like a drum machine. 'I didn't know it was you. How did you get here?'

'The front door was locked and the bell doesn't seem to work. No one came anyway. So I climbed up the drainpipe. The brickwork's so rotten you can kick foot-holes in it. Lucky this was your bedroom.'

Arthur wondered briefly how the other guests might have reacted to a strange girl tapping on their window in the middle of the night.

'And how did you get here, to the hotel?' he asked her.

She shrugged. 'Taxi.'

'But the roads are blocked.'

She laughed at that. 'Only outside your

161

window. They're clear up to the end of the drive. I had to walk from there. Your grandad gave me money for the taxi, which is just as well. I got a train to Clevedon, but it's still quite a way from there.'

Arthur was having trouble taking all this in. 'Hang on – you've seen Grandad?'

'Last night. After I rang, I couldn't think who else to go to.' She looked round. 'Anyway, where's your dad?'

'Back at home,' Arthur told her.

'If I'd known, I'd have gone to him instead.' She pulled herself up to sit cross-legged on the bed. Her jeans were wet from the snow, but she didn't seem to notice or care. 'Your grandad's nice, though, isn't he?' She looked straight at Arthur almost accusingly. 'Did you know he's Art? The Invisible Detective Art, I mean.'

Arthur nodded. 'Yes, I did. I've got his casebook, remember.' Somehow he had assumed she knew. Something else to discuss – if they ever found the time.

She nodded. 'Anyway, after I rang, I went to see him, to ask him what I should do.' She stopped talking and drummed her fingers on the bedcover.

'Let me back up a bit,' she decided. 'That holiday company – the one you told me about, that arranged all this? I looked them up on the web. Just out of interest really, and because Mum was asking.'

'So?'

'So,' she said, 'there's no such company.' She raised her eyebrows. 'You have been lured here under false pretences.'

'I know that,' Arthur said.

'You do?' She seemed disappointed. 'Oh.'

'I do now.' He told her quickly about the falling masonry, about the fire in the library and about finding the car under the snow. He related the events of the night – how someone had tried to break into his room.

'I must have given you a fright then,' she said. 'Sorry about that. I'm getting used to it. The woman at your grandad's nursing home wasn't too keen at being woken up at seven o'clock in the morning with stories of family emergencies. But I couldn't wait any longer. God knows what Mum thinks I'm up to. I left her a message that I was off to see Alison Potter. I hope she doesn't check.'

'All because you couldn't find the holiday company's website?' Arthur was glad she was here, now he had got over the shock. But it seemed an excessive response.

'Not just the website – no mention at all. I found this place, though.' She looked round the room. 'Bit of a dump, isn't it?'

'You're telling me.'

'So I rang up. I know it was the middle of the night, but I thought since it's a hotel they'd be used to that. International calls and stuff. I call Mum at all hours when she's in America. They don't seem to mind.'

'And you found out the phone's not working,' Arthur guessed.

She shook her head. 'It rang and rang. Eventually this husky voice answered.'

Of course, Arthur realised – the call he had heard in the middle of the night. The call that the person trying to break into his room had gone to answer.

'I wasn't daft enough to ask to talk to you,' Sarah was saying. 'I said you were staying there and could I leave you a message. I just wanted you to call and say you were OK and I was being stupid. You know?'

Arthur nodded.

'But this spooky voice told me to go away. It said there was no point in giving you a message. And I said, "Why not?"'

Arthur knew what was coming, but it still sent a shiver down his back.

'That's when I decided I'd go and see your grandad and ask him what to do. He told me to come here and check you were all right. Because the voice said there was no point giving you a message since you were already as good as dead.'

They just stared at each other for several moments. Then Sarah got up from the bed. She stood looking down at Arthur, her hands on her hips as if this was all somehow his fault.

'So what's going on?' she demanded.

Chapter 9

It was with some reluctance that Art's dad allowed the Cannoniers to accompany him and Charlie to the mirror maze. But the children were insistent, and Charlie pointed out that they could report back to Brandon Lake, whom the police were now keen to mollify after the attempted arrest.

'Besides,' Charlie added, 'there may be some simple trick to the murderer's disappearance that fresher, younger eyes will spot.' From the way Charlie looked at him, Art guessed that he had been impressed as well as amused by the disappearing trick he and Flinch had pulled off.

There was a policeman standing guard outside the art gallery, turning people away. The mirror maze poster outside had a piece of paper attached over it with drawing pins. It said: 'Closed Today'. As Art and the others ran up to the door, the policeman moved quickly to intercept them.

'It's all right, Rogers,' Art's dad informed him. 'They're with me.'

PC Rogers hesitated, evidently nonplussed, then stepped aside. 'Right you are, sir.'

Dad halted them in the foyer while he spoke briefly and quietly with another policeman. When he was finished he returned to where Art and the others were standing together with Charlie. 'The body's been removed,' he told them. 'In a minute I'll show you the scene of the crime.'

'What about the old lady?' Art wanted to know. He nodded to the doorway where the old woman who ran the attraction was still huddled into her coat behind the small table. 'She must have seen the murderer go in.'

'She did,' Art's dad said. 'She remembers because he was the only customer for a while. A hunched figure in a long coat. He said nothing, just dropped his coins in the tin and shambled into the maze.'

'Where he found and killed another customer,' Meg said.

Art's dad nodded. 'That's about the size of it.'

'But she saw him,' Jonny said excitedly. 'She saw the hunchback go in.'

'Yes,' Dad agreed. 'But the trouble is, she didn't see him come out again.'

'Then the answer would seem to be obvious,' Charlie said.

Art nodded. 'The killer,' he said, 'is still in there. Hiding in the maze.'

There was silence for a moment, interrupted by the polite cough of another policeman. 'Excuse me, sir,' he said to Arthur's dad, 'but the gentleman has given a statement and he's asking if he can go now.'

Dad frowned, then remembered. 'Oh, yes, the man who found the body.' He glanced at Charlie and the children. 'The man who raised the alarm. Though he didn't see the murderer. Have you been able to confirm his name and address?' he asked the policeman.

'I don't think that will be a problem,' a voice said. A tall man had come up behind the policeman. 'I think that Art here can vouch for me, if that will do.'

Art's dad was taken aback by this. 'Art?'

But Art was smiling. He recognised the man at once. 'This is Mr Sayers, Dad,' he said. 'He's staying at the Dog and Goose. We met the other day,' he added for his father's benefit.

'You were in the Dog?'

Mr Sayers came to Art's defence. 'We met outside the back of the pub,' he explained. 'Art was chatting to Bob the cellarman.'

Art's dad nodded. 'Yes, well, that seems to be in order, then. We know where to find you if we need any clarification of your statement.'

'Thank you. But I don't think there's much I can add to what I told you. I was looking round the maze. Getting rather lost, actually. Then I saw the poor gentleman slumped on the floor. Thought he was ill. But when I got to him, it was pretty obvious he was dead.'

'And you didn't see anyone else?' Art asked Sayers.

Sayers shook his head. 'Not a soul. Now, if you will excuse me, I have an appointment on the other side of town and I'm already running rather late.'

'I think you may be right,' Dad said to Art when Sayers had gone. 'The old lady didn't see the killer come out and we've had someone here from pretty much as soon as the body was found. No one has come out since. It was a nightmare trying to find the body even, let alone get it out again. So someone could still be in there, especially if they don't want to be found. The question is,' he told them, 'how do we go about searching for them to be sure we check every possible hiding place?'

It was Jonny who had the answer. 'Why don't you dismantle the maze? I mean, just take down the mirrors as you go through.'

'That's a good idea,' Charlie said. 'Then we shall just be left with a large empty room.'

'Could take a while,' Dad said. But Art could see that he was impressed with the idea.

'You don't have to bring all the mirrors out and dismantle everything,' Meg suggested. 'Just move them to the walls. The people who run the place will be able to set them back in position again pretty easily.'

'I'll ask the lady,' Dad said.

They worked methodically. Three police constables moved the mirrors, organised by Art's dad and Charlie, who had been given a plan of the maze by the old woman. She sat hunched at her table, watching through the door without comment.

Flinch sat on the floor at the back of the room. She had sneaked in when no one was looking, but before long Art, Jonny and Meg joined her.

'Do you think they'll find anyone?' Jonny asked.

'He can't just have vanished into thin air,' Meg said.

'Maybe he's running ahead of them,' Flinch said. 'That's what I'd do.'

Art agreed. 'In which case, he'll be behind one of the last mirrors they get to. I hope they're careful.'

'They seem to be,' Meg said.

The policemen had soon established a routine. Art's dad would point out which mirror was next to be moved. Two of the policemen then approached it from each side, trapping anyone who might be hiding behind the mirror. The third waited, in case the murderer made a run for it. Having established that nobody was there, the two either side of the mirror then lifted it and took it to the side of the room, where it was placed beside the other mirrors they had already moved. The third policeman again kept careful watch in case the killer tried to escape while his colleagues were busy.

As the room was cleared so the tension rose. Flinch could almost feel it in the air. The policemen were getting tired, but they were also becoming increasingly nervous. With fewer and fewer hiding places left, so it became more likely that the next mirror would be the one. That the killer would emerge from hiding at any moment. He might be armed with a knife, or a gun, or anything, Flinch thought. She shuffled closer to Art and he smiled reassuringly at her.

But she could see that Art was nervous now as well. Just two lines of mirrors to go. It was getting to the point where even Flinch would have been hard put to squeeze into the remaining possible hiding places.

One line. Now the police were moving slowly, glancing at each other and back at Art's dad and Charlie.

'Slowly,' Art's dad called. 'Take your time. There's no rush. Nearly there now.'

Art leaned across in front of Flinch to talk quietly to Jonny and Meg as well. 'Be ready,' he said. 'If the killer runs for it, he might just get past the police. Then it's up to us to stop him.'

Flinch shuddered at the thought. 'Jonny could follow him,' she said. 'See where he goes.'

Art nodded. 'If we can't stop him – or he's

armed – then that's the best bet. You up for it, Jonny?'

Jonny swallowed and nodded. He smiled thinly.

The police were moving along the last line of mirrors now. Just four more to go.

'This could be it,' Art's dad called. 'Easy now.'

It seemed to Flinch that everyone in the room was holding their breath. The policemen did not bother to move the mirrors. With just four of them left, there was no possibility of confusing reflections. They moved round to the other side of the mirrors and walked along. The distorting mirrors against the back wall of the room showed them variously as elongated stick-men and hunched, misshapen figures like the one they were hunting. But they also showed what the policemen had found: nothing at all.

There was nobody there.

The whole room seemed to breathe again as sighs of relief combined.

'He's gone,' Meg said. 'Somehow he got away.'

'He must have slipped past the old woman before the police got here,' Jonny said.

Art nodded. But he was frowning. 'What do you think, Flinch?'

Flinch was surprised but pleased to be asked. 'Me?' She thought about it. She stood up and looked round. There was nowhere left to hide. What would she do if someone was hunting for her in this room? 'I think,' she said, 'they should move those last mirrors. The funny ones.'

Art's dad and Charlie were within earshot now, walking despondently back across the large room.

'No one can get behind them,' Art's dad said. 'They're right up against the back wall.'

'There might be a door behind one of them. Hidden,' Flinch said. 'Or an alcove or something where you could squeeze in.'

Art's dad stopped in his tracks. He blinked, then he nodded. 'Yes, of course.' He sounded almost breathless at the thought. 'That must be it.'

He turned back to the policemen, who had heard this and were exchanging worried looks. One of them wiped his damp face with an enormous and not terribly clean handkerchief.

'You want us to move those last mirrors, sir?' one of the others asked.

Art's dad nodded.

'The big heavy ones?'

'Just enough to check behind them.'

'Do you think they'll find anything?' Meg asked as the policemen set to work again.

Art shook his head. 'No, I don't really think so. Flinch could maybe hide behind them, but not the killer. He's too big.'

'How do you know?' Art's dad asked. He was standing beside them, covering the doorway.

The policemen were moving the last of the distorting mirrors now, edging it cautiously away from the wall so they could check behind. One of them looked over towards where the children and Art's dad were waiting. 'Nothing,' he called. He sounded relieved rather than disappointed.

'Well,' Art confessed, 'I don't know how he does the disappearing act. But I do think I know who the killer is.'

Two of the policemen accompanied Art's dad, Charlie and the Cannoniers along the street to where the cage containing the performing apes was parked. The showman seemed to be between performances. The apes were in their cage – some sleeping on the straw strewn across the floor and a couple of them standing up, holding the bars. They watched Art and the others as if it was they and not the apes who were caged up and on display.

There was no sign of Tamworth the showman. Art's dad sent the policemen round to the other side of the cage – pushing past the showman's caravan as Art, Meg and Flinch had all done on various occasions before. They soon returned.

'It seems you might be right,' Charlie said to Art.

There was no sign of the enormous prize ape – the Mighty Kong. He was distinctive enough, and it was clear even before the policemen returned from checking the other side of the cage that he was not in there.

'You think it's escaped and not been reported?' Meg asked.

'Or it's been trained to commit the murders,' Art said. 'It can juggle and do sums. It wouldn't be difficult to instruct it to go to a certain place and kill whoever was there.'

'But it was enormous,' Jonny protested. 'Huge. Not a hunched figure like we saw.'

In reply, Art leaned forward, hunching his

shoulders and letting his arms dangle. Like an ape, he lumbered towards Jonny, who laughed despite himself.

'I agree,' Art's dad said. 'Put the thing in a long coat and a hat, and you'd have to get pretty close to realise it was an ape.' He shook his head. 'I walked right past this show the other night. Watched the thing go through its routine. Very intelligent and impressive – and, given the wrong sort of instruction, extremely dangerous, I imagine. Come on.'

He led the two policemen over to the showman's caravan. Art and the others crowded round too, trying to get a good view as Art's dad rapped on the door. There was no answer.

'There's a window at the back,' Flinch called out suddenly.

'Break the door down,' Charlie said urgently. 'Before the man escapes.'

One of the policemen prepared to put his shoulder to it, but Art's father simply turned the handle and pulled the door open. It had not been locked.

The scene that was revealed inside the caravan was bizarre to say the least. Most of the space in the tiny room was taken up with a small table. Along one side was a couch that served as a bed. Sitting on the couch was the showman, a half-finished glass of beer on the table in front of him.

'What the devil?' he said in surprise and anger as the door swung open.

Next to the showman, also sitting at the table, was another figure. A larger figure, silhouetted against the light filtering through the window at the back of the caravan. It also turned as the door opened.

The Mighty Kong – the prize ape. It froze at the sight of the people crowded into the doorway. It was holding a glass of beer to its mouth and seemed to splutter into it in surprise.

As Art's dad stepped into the small caravan, the ape seemed to catch sight of the uniformed policemen behind him.

'Cor, 'strewth,' the huge ape said out loud. 'It's the law.' And with that, it set down its glass of beer and leaped out of the window.

Arthur wore his coat down to breakfast. He took it off and hung it over the back of the chair when he sat down. Then he made sure he took two bread rolls as well as extra toast at breakfast. He wrapped them in paper napkins and stuffed them into his coat pockets.

He was the first down that Sunday morning and left just as Mr Huntingdon was arriving. The portly man stopped him in the doorway, fixing him with a piercing stare, his bulky form preventing Arthur from leaving.

'Did you sleep well?' he asked.

Arthur was not quite sure what to say. He mumbled something about the bed being rather hard and managed to push past.

'That's what I thought,' Mr Huntingdon replied.

But Arthur wasn't listening. He was already hurrying up the stairs, his coat packed with Sarah's breakfast.

* * *

They spent an hour talking through what had happened to Arthur – from the attempted abduction outside school to the events of the previous night. Arthur also told Sarah about Mr Huntingdon's enquiry about how he had slept.

'Maybe he's just curious,' Sarah said.

'*Too* curious,' Arthur thought. 'He's been poking his nose into everything all weekend. I've seen him sneaking about all over the place. He's up to something.'

'But murder?'

Arthur shrugged. The whole thing was so incredible. Could someone really be trying to kill him? Had they gone to the trouble of inventing a fictitious company to lure him on a holiday at this remote house so they could murder him? Why? And if they had, then what was the point of trying to abduct him from school just before he was due to come here anyway?

'None of this makes any sense,' he told Sarah.

She shrugged. 'You mean, we can't make sense of it. That's not the same.'

'So how do we make sense of it?'

'I don't know.'

The room was getting Arthur down. It seemed

small and cramped and suddenly stuffy. 'I need some air,' he said.

Sarah smiled. 'We could climb down the drainpipe.'

'Bit difficult to explain if anyone sees us,' Arthur decided, not sure if she was being serious. 'Easier and safer just to creep out. If anyone sees you, say you work here. Making the beds or something.'

But no one did see them. The only time Arthur was worried was as they dashed past the dining-room door. Inside he could hear Mr Smith talking loudly. He did not look to see who else was there. Mr Huntingdon would have finished and gone by now. Mrs Trefusis probably took breakfast in her room. Mr Peters might be fussing round and telling everyone how good the toast was while Miss Napier did the real work.

And Mr Ashe, the stranded motorist, Arthur thought, would be staring gloomily at his scrambled eggs and wondering how he was ever going to get to some meeting or other and what to do about the meetings he had already missed.

But in this at least Arthur was very wrong.

* * *

'Don't look now,' Sarah said quietly, 'but someone's watching us.'

Arthur did look, of course. There was a tall, thin figure standing in the shadows a short way off. From the way he was peering between the low, snow-laden branches of one of the trees, he did not realise they had seen him.

'It's Bill,' he whispered to Sarah. 'The groundsman.'

But Sarah's attention was already elsewhere. 'What's that? On the ground?'

There was a small clearing in front of them, just within the treeline. In the middle of the clearing was a dark shape. It looked like a low mound of dark earth breaking through the carpet of white. But when they got closer, they could see that it was a man. Lying in the snow.

'Mr Ashe,' Arthur said in surprise.

The man did not move. But on the other side of the clearing, Bill the groundsman turned and ran.

'You'd think he'd come and help, not scarper,' Sarah said with obvious contempt.

Arthur was kneeling beside Mr Ashe. The man's eyes were closed and his skin was cold and almost as pale as the snow. 'Perhaps he already knows there's nothing anyone can do,' Arthur said.

'What?' Sarah crouched down beside him, shook the body by the shoulder, trying to wake him.

Arthur gently stopped her. 'It's no good,' he said quietly. 'He's dead.'

Chapter 10

'So I didn't imagine it,' Meg declared. She had heard the Mighty Kong speak before, though she had dismissed it as fantasy or imagination

There was little time to be amazed at the fact that the ape was drinking beer with the showman and still less to wonder at its sudden powers of speech.

Art's father recovered first. 'Stay here – with him,' he told one of the policemen, motioning for him to stay with the showman. 'You,' he told the other, 'come with me. Let's find that monkey.'

They were out of the caravan and running along the street in a moment. But Meg and the others could see as well as Art's dad and the policeman that there was no sign of the ape.

'You'd think he'd attract some attention,' Charlie said, catching up with them. 'Listen and see if you can hear any shouts or cries from people at the fair. An ape running amok will excite some interest.'

'No sign,' Art's dad admitted as he returned. The policeman was checking further along the street, but there was no way the ape could have got that far without them seeing. 'Vanished into thin air again.'

'Maybe he doubled back,' Jonny thought. 'Round the other side of the cage.'

Charlie shook his head. 'I've been watching. And anyway, we would have heard a commotion. There are a lot of people over at that end of the street.'

Art was looking thoughtful. He was tapping his finger against his chin in a way which Meg knew meant he had had an idea.

'What is it?' she asked.

'I don't think this vanishing act is quite so hard to fathom out, that's all.' He grinned. 'Flinch and I know where the ape went. Don't we?' he said to Flinch.

Her eyes widened with realisation. 'Yes. Where we hid from the showman.'

The second policeman had brought the hapless Tamworth out from his caravan and led him over as well. The man was mumbling and cursing under his breath. Art led them round to the cage.

'He's underneath,' Flinch told them. 'That's where me and Art hid.'

The showman's lip curled. 'Thought I'd seen you before. Was it you who tried to break into my cage?'

'No, it wasn't,' Art told him firmly.

Art's dad was down on his hands and knees. He stood up, dusting his palms. 'He's under there all right, trying to hide behind the wheel.' He turned to the showman. 'If you can control him, call him out.'

The showman considered for a moment. Then he shrugged. 'Ain't a crime,' he said. 'Just a bit of fun.'

'A bit of fun?' Charlie echoed, incredulous. 'Murder – a bit of fun?'

'Murder?' Now it was the showman's turn to show surprise. 'Now wait a minute . . .' He looked from Charlie to Art's father to the policeman. Then he swallowed and called under the cage. 'It's all right, Fred. I think you'd better come out here.'

'Fred?' Meg said. 'I thought it was Mighty Kong.'

'Well, that's his stage name. I can't call him Fred in front of the crowd, now can I?'

The ape was hauling itself from under the cage. When it stood, it was surprisingly upright.

Its arms were not hanging low as usual and its shoulders were squared rather than hunched.

'So,' the ape said, 'what gives?'

By way of answer, Art reached up and grabbed the ape's nose. Meg gasped. She was sure that the animal would go for him – that in a moment Art would be sprawled bleeding on the pavement.

But she was wrong. Instead, Art tugged at the nose and the ape's whole face seemed to pull away. Beneath the mask was revealed the red, perspiring face of a young man. His dark hair was streaked damply across his forehead.

'The other apes are real,' the showman was saying. 'But who's going to pay to see a few monkeys pacing up and down? We need tricks and performance, don't we, Fred? We need to make a living. Keep the apes fed and watered and in straw. Doesn't hurt. No harm done. It's a living.'

'So this is Fred?' Art's dad said slowly.

'My boy, that's right.'

Fred was nodding too. He still had the ape-costume headpiece on like the hood of a coat.

'And where was Fred . . .' Art's dad checked his watch. 'Where was he an hour and forty minutes ago?'

The showman frowned. 'He was here. With me. We were doing our first performance of the evening.' He paused to glare at Fred. 'And discovering, by the by, that four plus three makes six. Weren't we, Fred?'

Fred hung his head and said nothing, while one of the policemen was dispatched to find people at the fair who had witnessed the performance and could vouch for the Mighty Kong's presence during the act.

'All right,' Art's dad said after hearing several witnesses confirm that the 'ape' had indeed performed. He was addressing the hapless Fred. 'I could probably have you for trading under false pretences or something. But be off with you – go on.' He turned to Art and the others. 'It was a good idea, but it seems we still have to find our killer.' He nodded to the policeman. 'You and I had better go and round up some people to help put that mirror maze back together or they'll be sending Scotland Yard a bill for loss of earnings.'

The policeman sighed audibly, and the two of them headed back towards the gallery.

Charlie lingered a little longer. 'An interesting evening, as ever,' he said with a smile.

'But I'm afraid it doesn't help us find the murderer, as Sergeant Drake pointed out. Maybe,' he went on, winking at Art and the others, 'he really does vanish into thin air. Just like Brandon Lake.' Then he touched his hat politely, nodded to the showman and headed back down the street into the fair.

Meg was about to suggest they make their way back to the den. She had had enough of the fair for now. But then she caught sight of Art's expression. 'What is it, Art?'

Art looked at her. His mouth was hanging open. 'I just thought of something.'

'What?' Jonny demanded.

'Just like Brandon Lake. That's what Charlie said.'

'But that was us,' Flinch said, glancing at the showman, who was still standing with them. He seemed to be preoccupied with his apes – staring into the cage and clicking his tongue, as if trying to communicate with them.

'What are you thinking?' Meg wanted to know. 'What do you mean?'

'I'm not sure,' Art admitted. 'Just an idea for now. I need to work it out in my head.' He approached the showman, tapping him on the shoulder when the man ignored him.

'What is it? You've caused me enough trouble.'

'Yes, I'm sorry. But you mentioned someone tried to break into the cage.'

The showman nodded. 'I thought it was you, when I saw you the other night and you were pulling at the bars.'

'It wasn't us,' Flinch insisted.

'No. Don't reckon it was. I reckon it was that bloke that tried to buy one of the apes off me.'

'Someone tried to buy the Mighty Kong?' Meg said. 'I mean, Fred?'

'No, not him. One of the other apes. Any of the other apes, he said.' The showman turned back to the cage. 'Offered a lot of money. But, well, I couldn't part with any of them. Goodness knows what he wanted an ape for. Could have been anything.'

'So you think he came back and tried to steal one of them?' Jonny asked.

'Seems likely.'

'And this man,' Art said slowly, 'did he mention his name?'

The showman nodded without looking round. 'Don't remember what it was, though. Edward something, I think.'

Art nodded. The shadows of the cage bars cut across his face, threw it into darkness. But Meg could see that his expression was grave. 'Was it Edward Sayers?'

The showman turned, surprised. 'Yes,' he said. 'That's right. How could you know that? Edwards Sayers – that was his name.'

But Art was gone, was already running back down the street into the fair. Jonny set off after him. Meg hesitated only a second, then she took Flinch's hand and the two girls ran after them, towards the Dog and Goose.

They felt for a pulse, listened for a heartbeat, held wet fingers in front of Mr Ashe's mouth. But they could find no breath, no signs of life.

'I told you,' Arthur said quietly.

'There must be something we can do,' Sarah protested.

'It's too late.'

'Maybe that groundsman went for help.'

Arthur grunted. 'Maybe.' But why hadn't he told them there was a dead body lying in the snow, Arthur wondered? He must have seen it – just as he had certainly seen Sarah and himself. He looked round, hoping to catch sight of Bill waiting somewhere nearby.

What he saw was a building – a low wooden building almost hidden among the trees deeper in the wood.

Sarah followed Arthur's gaze and she could see it too. 'Perhaps there's someone there. We can get help. It's closer than the hotel.'

'Do you think one of us should stay here?' Arthur asked. It didn't seem right just to leave the man lying there.

I think we should stick together,' Sarah said softly.

'Oh?'

'Haven't you noticed?' She rolled the man's head slightly to one side and now Arthur could see dark brown clots of blood. 'He didn't just collapse from a heart attack or anything.'

'Why isn't there more blood?' was all that

Arthur could think to say. He felt cold, as if the snow was getting inside his body and chilling him from the inside out. 'Come on, then.'

They set off slowly towards the wooden building. It was little more than a large shed, Arthur saw, as they approached. It had a felted roof, though that was all but covered in snow, and a single window in the side. The window was clear plastic, but was so scratched and grubby that it was impossible to see anything inside.

The door was latched but not locked. A padlock was hanging open on the clasp and Arthur removed it, opened the clasp, then replaced the padlock as it had been. He pulled at the door and they stepped inside.

It was obviously the groundsman's hut. One wall was lined with hooks from which hung various pieces of gardening equipment and tools: spade, fork, shovel, hoe. There was a short scythe and a billhook. Plastic flowerpots were stacked up in a corner, next to bags of fertiliser. A small tractor with lawnmower blades attached to it was parked haphazardly in the middle of the shed.

The wall opposite the tools was taken up with a long dresser unit. The wood was scarred and stained and some of the drawers were half open.

'Hello!' Sarah called. But it was apparent that there was nobody there. She sighed. 'I think we'd better head back for the hotel, don't you?'

But Arthur's attention was taken up with something else. The door had swung back shut behind them. When he turned to open it, he saw that there was a hook on the back of the door. And hanging on the hook was a coat. It was a coat he recognised.

'Look at this.'

'It's just an overcoat.'

'It's the one the man who tried to kidnap me was wearing.' He was sure of it.

Sarah was less convinced. She lifted a sleeve and examined it before letting it drop back into place. 'Similar,' she conceded.

But Arthur was not to be put off. He reached into the pocket and felt around. Nothing. The other pocket . . . In this one there was something, something that scratched at his hand. He pulled it out, unrolling it. Some sort of material, dark and bristling.

It was a false beard.

They looked at it for a while in silence.

Then Arthur stuffed it back into the pocket.

'He said he was the chauffeur as well as the groundsman,' Arthur recalled. 'So he'd have the use of the car I found. Convinced?'

'Convinced.' Sarah turned and looked back into the main part of the shed. 'Let's see what else we can find.'

'Do you think we should?' Arthur began to protest. He reckoned the best course of action was to leave while no one knew they had been here. Besides, there was a murder to report, though with the phones not working he wasn't sure what could be done about that.

Sarah had different ideas. She was pulling open the doors in the lower part of the dresser, checking inside each one, then pushing them shut again. Arthur joined her, following along and looking into the drawers above. String, secateurs, screwdrivers, a penknife . . .

They were almost at the end when Sarah gave a low whistle and stepped back. The double doors of the cupboard she was checking were wide open. Inside, Arthur could see a mass of glassware – tubes and containers, beakers and pipettes. It looked like something out of the science lab at school. He remembered the chemistry books in the library.

'What's going on here?' he wondered out loud.

'Some sort of distillation?' Sarah pointed to a glass jar at the end of the cupboard. A tube was positioned above it, so that something would drip out and into the jar. 'They collect something in here, by the look of it. Like in chemistry.'

'But what?'

Sarah shrugged and pushed the doors closed.

Arthur moved to open the two drawers above that cupboard. The first was empty save for a box of matches, a ball of twine and some plastic plant labels. The second drawer too was almost empty.

Almost. Inside was a glass vial — like a small medicine bottle with a cork for a stopper. As Arthur took it out and held it up, they could both see the viscous red liquid inside. It adhered lazily to the sides of the vial as Arthur tipped it gently to and fro, running slowly down the glass.

'It looks like blood,' Sarah said.

Arthur was about to agree. But at that moment the door of the shed burst open and a tall figure stood framed in the doorway. With a snarl of rage, Bill slammed the door behind him and stalked menacingly towards them.

Chapter 11

It was when Charlie had mentioned Brandon Lake's mysterious disappearance that Art realised how it must be done. Jonny, Meg and Flinch caught up with him as he approached the Dog and Goose.

'So what's going on?' Jonny wanted to know.

'Where are we going?' Meg demanded.

'Have you solved it?' Flinch asked.

'I want to search Mr Sayers's room above the pub,' Art told them.

'That's illegal,' Meg said sternly.

'We could just have a look round,' Jonny said. But he sounded nervous at the prospect.

'No one would know,' Flinch pointed out.

'No,' Meg said.

They all stopped and looked at her. She was standing with her arms folded, the glow of a nearby streetlight making her hair glow like fire.

'Not until Art tells us why he thinks that Mr Sayers is behind all this.'

Art nodded. 'That's fair,' he agreed. 'And I warn you, I don't have proof. But I just don't see how else it could be done.'

'So tell us,' Jonny urged.

Art set off again and they walked quickly to keep up. 'It was Sayers who tried to buy an ape and who then tried to steal one. I don't know why, but that proves he's up to no good.'

'Go on,' said Meg. She did not yet sound convinced.

'The attacker – killer now – is apparently a small, hunched figure who disappears.'

'We know that,' Meg said.

'So think back to the trick that Flinch and I played. Because I think our killer is playing the same trick, but in reverse.'

'You mean there's two of them dressed up?' Flinch said. Her face was crumpled into a frown as she tried to work this out and Art laughed.

'Not quite. But when the police were looking for Brandon Lake, they found two children instead. They assumed that the Invisible Detective had lived up to his name and vanished. But we know he hadn't. He was still there, but they didn't see him. Or rather, they didn't realise they'd seen him.'

'And Sayers was at the scene of the crime,' Jonny said. 'Is that the point?'

'Sort of. Nobody asked the old woman if she had seen him go in. Just the hunched figure they were expecting. But I think, if they had asked, the police would have found that nobody remembered Mr Sayers going into the mirror maze. Only coming out again.'

'And the murderer went in, but didn't come out,' Meg said slowly, 'because . . .' She could see it, Art was sure, but she didn't yet quite believe it.

'Because just as Brandon Lake and Flinch and I are one and the same, so Mr Sayers and the Hunchback of Cricklewood are the same person!'

They were at the end of the alley behind the Dog and Goose now. 'Remember when we lost the hunchback – he was here and then he wasn't.'

'But Mr Sayers was,' Jonny remembered. 'He said no one else had come into the alley.'

'And he was telling the truth,' Art said. 'As Meg could have told us if she had been there.' He crouched down low suddenly, hunching his shoulders and letting his arms hang down. Doubled up like this, Art was at Flinch's eye level and he winked at her. 'You be the victim, Flinch.'

'All right.' She grinned. 'Do I have to scream or anything?'

'No, that might attract attention. Just stand there and I'll pretend to murder you.'

Flinch stood absolutely still and Art the hunchback made a pretence of strangling her. He paused to look back over his shoulder. 'Now, what if someone comes along – Meg and Jonny, say? The hunchback runs off.' At this, Art ran – a lolloping, lurching, rolling movement – until he was hidden behind the empty barrels stacked against the wall of the alley.

'And we chase after him,' Jonny realised, leading the others round to where Art was now standing upright. 'And here he is.'

'Ah, but he isn't, is he?' Art countered. 'I'm not a hunchback. I'm Mr Sayers – very tall and upstanding and not at all sinister. And I can honestly say that I saw no one else hiding behind these barrels.'

'That easy?' Meg said. She still sounded dubious.

'That easy,' Art assured her. 'Think how easy it was for us to fool the police with Brandon Lake. And in the mirror maze, a hunched figure goes in and Mr Sayers comes out to raise the alarm.'

'But how do we prove it?' Jonny wanted to

know. 'I mean, the theory is fine. But the police will need proof.'

Art nodded. 'Which is why I want to look in his room.'

'And what if he's in there?' Meg demanded. 'Will you just ask him if he's the killer?'

'He's not in there,' Flinch said. 'He told us he had to be on the other side of London, remember?'

Meg had to admit that Art's theory made sense, so she agreed: 'But just a quick look round, and if we find anything we get the police.' Any further protest she might have made was dispelled by her concealed amusement at Jonny's annoyance that he was left to keep watch.

'Why can't Flinch keep watch?' he wanted to know. 'Or Meg? She doesn't want to go up there anyway.'

The conversation was conducted in a whisper on the stairs up to the rooms above the pub. The door had been locked, but with an open skylight above, it was easy for Art to hoist Flinch on to his shoulders and then she squeezed through the narrow space to unlock the door for them.

'You're the fastest, Jonny,' Art insisted. 'So if someone comes, you can get up the stairs and warn us quicker than anyone else. You're just the best man for the job.'

Reluctantly Jonny was forced to agree. 'Tell me what you find,' he hissed as the others tiptoed up the stairs.

'We won't find anything,' Meg assured him. 'Murderers don't go leaving clues lying round their rooms.'

But she was soon proved wrong.

Sayers had two rooms above the pub, joined by a connecting door. The lights were on and they could see at once that the first was simply a bedroom. It was quite spacious, with bare wooden floorboards, a chest of drawers, an upright chair and a wardrobe. A window gave out on to the alleyway.

The door to the other room was standing ajar and Flinch ran over to take a look. 'Over here,' she called excitedly. 'What's all this stuff?'

The three of them went through to find themselves in a small sitting room. But the furniture had been pushed to the walls. Only a small dining table remained in the centre of the room. It was piled high with glassware – flasks and tubes and beakers and pipes. A candle stood under one flask, its flame blackening the underside of the glass while a dark liquid bubbled away gently. Steam rose from the liquid and travelled along the tubes and pipes before condensing in another jar. Then the process was repeated. At the end of the table a dark, red liquid dripped slowly into a final flask.

'Like a mad scientist's laboratory from a film,' Art breathed.

'Someone's spilled something,' Flinch said. She scraped at a patch of floorboard at the end of the table where there was a dark stain.

'I don't like it,' Meg confessed. 'I don't know what it is, but let's get out of here.'

'I agree,' Art said, much to Meg's relief. 'I don't know what's going on here either. But I think we've seen enough. Let's go and get some help.'

The three of them all but ran back into the small bedroom. Meg was in the lead and was reaching for the door when it opened towards her. She gasped, her hand flying to her chest in fright.

It was Jonny.

'You scared the life out of me,' she told him, slapping his arm.

But Jonny's face was serious. 'Someone's coming,' he said. 'I heard them on the stairs.'

'Sayers?' Art asked.

Jonny shook his head. 'Don't know. Maybe.'

'Hide!' Flinch hissed. In a moment she was out of sight – crammed into the space behind the curtains, though Meg would never have guessed there was room.

'She's right,' Art said. Jonny was already diving under the bed. Art followed him.

Meg looked round. There was not enough room under the bed for her as well. But she could see nowhere else to go. The other room offered no hiding places and she could hear the scrape of footsteps approaching up the stairs. She stood frozen in front of the door.

'Wardrobe!' a voice hissed. It was Art, his head sticking out from under the bed. 'Try the wardrobe!' Then he disappeared again.

Meg ran quickly to the wardrobe and pulled one of the double doors open. It was easily large enough and she stepped inside, pulling the door closed behind her and burrowing into the coats and jackets that were hanging inside.

There was a crack of light where the doors did not quite meet. Just enough for Meg to be able to peep out into the room and see if anyone did come in. Just enough for her to see her own feet if she looked down. Just enough for her to become aware that there was a pair of shoes in the wardrobe, positioned beside her feet. Ladies' shoes, she realised.

As her eyes adjusted to the near-darkness, she saw that they were not just shoes. There were legs as well. Someone was standing beside her in the wardrobe. Someone had been hiding in there already when she got in.

Cautiously, not wanting to but somehow having to, Meg eased the coats aside. Eyes stared back at her out of the gloom. But they were blank and unseeing. The young woman beside Meg was perhaps twenty, probably not yet that. She was not standing, but had been propped up, wedged in place to stop her falling.

And her eyes, like the rest of her, were quite, quite dead.

Meg screamed. She shoved the door open and leaped out of the wardrobe.

She was vaguely aware that Jonny and Art were pulling themselves out from under the bed to see what was happening. Out of the corner of her eye she saw Flinch pull back the curtain. But she had already turned back to watch as, with horrific inevitability, the body of what must be Elsie the barmaid fell forwards out of the wardrobe.

Behind her, another door crashed open. Meg turned sharply, hand to her mouth in terror. She was just in time to see a hunched, misshapen figure lurch unsteadily into the room.

Arthur thought that Bill was going to attack him. But as they approached he seemed to stagger, then collapse to the floor. He sat with his back against the side of the small tractor, moaning quietly.

Sarah looked at Arthur and he shrugged.

'Why did you have to come?' Bill was whimpering. 'Why?'

'What are you talking about?' Arthur said. 'You tried to bring me here by force.'

'We know it was you,' Sarah said. 'We found the beard and the coat.'

Bill looked up at them, his eyes wide and watery. 'I wanted to warn you. Make sure you didn't come. It's all starting up again now.'

'And what about this?' Arthur snapped. He didn't know what it was, but he yanked open the drawer and held up the vial of viscous liquid. Then he pushed open the cupboard doors to reveal the strange equipment. 'How do you explain this lot away, then?'

'Not mine,' Bill insisted. His whole body was shaking. But he made an effort to gather himself and lurched unsteadily to his feet. 'I didn't know it was there, not until I found out about how Arthur Drake was back.'

'What about Arthur Drake?' Sarah demanded.

Bill was staring across at Arthur, his eyes red-rimmed and angry. 'Arthur Drake,' he snarled. 'It's all your fault. If you hadn't come back. Hadn't been seen.'

'What's he on about?' Sarah said.

Arthur shook his head. 'No idea.'

'No idea?' Bill laughed – a snort of humourless sound. 'Don't you get it yet? Can't you see this is all for your benefit? All set up to get you here?'

'We know that,' Sarah hissed. 'But why?'

'To kill him of course,' Bill said. 'That's what this is all about. Finally – the death of Arthur Drake.'

He wiped his face on his sleeve. His eyes seemed to have lost their fire and he leaned against the dresser. 'I tried to stop it. I tried to save you. I thought I could frighten you off by pushing the stone from the wall. Why couldn't you stay away?'

Arthur's mind was in a whirl. Bill had pushed the stone to save him – to scare him away? 'I don't know what you're talking about,' he said. 'Who is trying to kill me? And why? What have I done?

Bill met his gaze, just for a moment, then he looked away. 'All right,' he said. 'I'll tell you.' He looked back at Arthur, his face set – grim and determined. 'You may not believe the half of it, but I'll tell you everything.'

Chapter 12

Jonny disappeared back under the bed. Art did not hesitate. He pulled himself out and to his feet, running to comfort Meg. He put his arm round her shoulder and held her tight. He tried not to look down at the body of the woman, which was thankfully lying face-down.

The figure in the doorway took an uncertain step forwards. It had to twist its head awkwardly to look across at Meg and Art. There was something familiar about the eyes, Art realised, something in the way the skin was stretched over the ugly face and lipless mouth. Something about the figure's whole posture and demeanour.

It took another faltering step into the room. 'Help me,' the hunched figure said, its voice brittle.

In that moment, Art realised what that something familiar was. 'Mr Sayers?'

The head dropped and the hunched figure stared at the floor. It shambled another couple of steps and now it was looking down at the body lying beside Art and Meg.

'Poor Elsie,' the voice crackled. 'I thought I

was safe, locked in here. Until the cravings, the feelings, burned themselves out. But then Elsie came in to change the sheets . . .' The misshapen body was shaking back and forth, and Art realised with a shock that it was sobbing with remorse.

'What happened to you?' Meg said.

Art could hear the nervous catch in her voice.

The hunched figure straightened slightly at the sound of her voice. 'Nothing,' it said emphatically. 'I was born like this.' Again the head angled so that the eyes were staring at the two children. 'There is no Edward Sayers. Only me.'

Behind the figure, Art could see Jonny emerging from the other side of the bed. Flinch had stepped out from behind the curtain. Her face was a picture of sympathy and Art was afraid she was about to say something, to give herself away. He frowned, nodding towards the door, hoping either Flinch or Jonny would understand.

Jonny seemed to. He pointed to the door, eyebrows raised, questioning. Again Art nodded, hoping that Sayers – if it really was Sayers – would not notice and turn to look. But he was again staring down at the body of Elsie. Behind him, Jonny took Flinch by the hand and led her quietly to the door. He paused just long enough to mouth to Art and Meg, 'We'll get help.' Then Jonny was gone, following Flinch quietly down the stairs.

'I killed her.' The voice was strained with tears now. 'I could not stop myself. When the feeling comes, I can't control it.'

Meg was tugging at Art's arm. She pulled him back, round the bed. Sayers was between them and the door, but they could get to the window while he seemed distracted. It was already open a few inches. Art put his hands under it and pushed. The window opened a few inches more, but not nearly enough. Then it stopped, refusing to budge. Jammed, or perhaps it simply did not open more than that – to stop people climbing in. Or out.

As soon as they reached the turn of the stairs, Jonny and Flinch ran. Jonny reached the door out into the alleyway first. There was another door, through to the pub. But it might be locked and anyway Jonny did not want to have to explain what he was doing breaking into the guests' rooms. Better to head back for the mirror maze and hope Art's dad was still there, putting the mirrors back where they should be.

The alley was in near-darkness. Jonny spared a glance back up at the window that he now knew gave into Mr Sayers's room – a patch of light in the dark of the brickwork. He thought he saw the window move, open slightly, but it was difficult to tell from this angle.

Flinch was calling to him to hurry. So Jonny ran on, catching up with her easily.

Then they both skidded to a halt as someone stepped out of the darkness ahead of them. Flinch gave a shriek of surprise.

'You!' Jonny said in disbelief.

The hunchback was watching them trying desperately to open the window, though he made no effort to stop them. 'I was born like this,' he said again. 'And if only I had accepted it, if only I had been strong enough, that would have been the end of the matter.'

'What happened?' Art asked, giving up on the window.

Meg nervously took hold of his hand again.

But somehow he thought they were in no immediate danger.

'We found a way to cure the affliction. A way that I could be normal. Not stared at like some fairground attraction.'

'What went wrong?' Art asked quietly.

The sad eyes lifted once more to stare at Art and Meg. 'The potion, the cure . . . It is made from human blood.' With a snarl of rage and anguish, Sayers turned away. 'And when I am in the form of Edward Sayers – the handsome, healthy gentleman – I cannot bear the thought of reverting to . . . to . . .' For a moment he was unable to bring himself to say it. 'To this!' he eventually spat. 'Even when I am back to normal – to what is normal for me – even then I cannot control the cravings. I have to get blood, to mix more potion.' He was looking again at the body. 'And so Elsie died.'

'And that's why you attacked the old man in the alley. And killed the man at the mirror maze,' Meg said. Her voice was angry rather than frightened now.

'I cannot control these urges.' He did not look at them. 'I ran away, tried to escape, to think for myself. I thought that alone I could fight it. But it is too late now. I had hoped the blood of an ape might be a substitute, but I could neither buy nor steal one to find out.' Sayers shook his hanging head sadly, then turned back towards them. 'You should go now,' he said quietly. 'Before the sickness takes me again. In moments of weakness, it comes over me very swiftly.'

Art nodded, leading Meg towards the door. But before they reached it, the door began to swing open. Instinctively, they backed away, towards the window again. But Sayers lurched forwards and pulled at the door.

It was Old Toby, the dog. He limped into the room, glanced at Art and Meg, then hobbled painfully across the room, towards the door into the makeshift laboratory.

'He seems to know his way around,' Art said. Sayers was blocking their path to the door now, although he seemed calm and safe enough.

'He came in while I was distilling the potion,' Sayers said. 'Got under my feet, so I dropped a whole batch.' There was a crackle that might have been laughter. 'He lapped it up, every last drop.'

'We saw the stain on the floor,' Meg said.

'And he changed too, didn't he?' Art said, realising.

'Oh, yes. He changed. Like me, he became young and virile and strong again. It can make you young, you know. That was what . . .' He stepped away from the door. 'Now Old Toby returns to lick at the floorboards in the hope that a few drops remain. He too has a craving for energy and youth. But it would be wrong of me to feed it.' Sayers stopped abruptly. His head snapped up to look at them. 'You must go,' he said urgently. 'Go now. Before it takes me again. I can feel it rising inside me.' His eyes glinted darkly in the lamplight. 'Go now!'

'This is Miss Waters,' Jonny told Flinch. 'She's looking for her brother.'

'And I believe I have found him,' the young woman said. 'He is here, above the Dog and Goose.' She was clutching a small handbag.

'You mean Mr Sayers?' Jonny said.

'There's only the hunchback up there now,' Flinch said. She was keeping Jonny between herself and the woman.

'Hunchback?' the woman snapped. 'Where?'

'Up in Mr Sayers's room. Our friends are up there too.'

'With the hunchback?'

Jonny nodded. 'We managed to escape.'

'The hunchback will kill my brother,' Miss Waters said. She was walking slowly along the alley. 'He will say anything to discredit him.' She turned sharply towards Jonny and Flinch. 'You mustn't believe a word that creature says.' She grabbed Jonny by the shoulders. 'You hear me?'

He nodded. 'Yes. We were going for the police. To get help.'

'You're right.' She let go of Jonny. 'Your friends are in terrible danger. But there's no time for the police. We have to help them now.'

'Jonny can run really fast,' Flinch said.

But in reply Miss Waters pointed up at the window. From where they were, further down the alley than when Jonny had last looked, they could see into the room. The light threw silhouettes of the people inside against the window. Jonny could see the shadowy forms of Meg and Art backing away across the room.

And rising up in front of them a hunched, distorted figure seemed to grow and change into

216

the shape of a tall, thin man. Its perfectly formed hands extended threateningly in front as it advanced on the cowering shapes of Art and Meg. From the open window came a girl's shriek of terror.

Having decided that he was prepared to tell Arthur and Sarah what was happening, Bill seemed to gather himself. He took a deep breath and stood up. He was swaying slightly on his feet, perhaps still uncertain that he had made the right decision.

'Well?' Arthur prompted.

'It was an accident,' Bill said. He sounded apologetic. 'Just coincidence. We were driving back from London, from the City, and we just happened to pass the school as you were leaving.' He leaned heavily on the dresser. 'The traffic was bad of course. End of school. Usual chaos, I suppose. We slowed right down.' He looked at Art, his eyes large and sad. 'And there you were. Arthur Drake.' He shook his head. 'I thought if I came back and warned you, made you listen, you might believe me. But you ran off before I could warn you.'

'But why?' Arthur struggled to make sense of it. 'Why me? What's so important about me?'

But he got no answer.

The shed door smashed open. A tall figure blotted out the brilliance of the snow outside. In a sudden whirl, it rushed across the space between them.

Bill turned at the sound. He opened his mouth to say something, but the dark figure lashed out, sending him sprawling against the dresser. He slipped and fell, his head cracking on the wooden edge and snapping backwards. He collapsed with a grunt and was still.

But the figure that had knocked him down was a blur of movement, arms flailing. Arthur got only a confused impression of a large overcoat with turned-up collar. A wide-brimmed hat pulled down low. An incredibly strong arm sending him flying into Sarah, so they both fell heavily to the floor.

The shadowy figure swept past, scooping the vial of red liquid from the dresser. Then it turned and ran from the shed.

Arthur helped Sarah to her feet. She bent over, winded, retching the air back into her body. Bill was breathing heavily, but his eyes were closed. Out cold, Arthur realised. He ran to the shed door.

There was no sign of the person that had attacked them. But a line of scuffed footprints led clearly through the snow – back into the woods and towards the hotel.

'Come on.' Sarah was beside him now. 'Follow the footprints. We came the other way, so they're not ours.'

'Could be Bill's,' Arthur pointed out as they ran.

Sarah was shaking her head, her long black hair catching in the breeze as she ran, swirling round her like in a shampoo advert. 'No way. He came from the clearing like us. From that body.'

Arthur had all but forgotten the body. But he remembered it now – alone and cold and dead in the snow. They were following a murderer.

At the edge of the wood, the tracks led straight back to the front door of the hotel, lost on the way among others that crossed and recrossed – Arthur's, Sarah's, probably the unfortunate Mr Ashe's.

'We have to tell someone,' Arthur gasped as they slowed to a walk.

'But who can we trust? Should we go for help? Try to get to the nearest village or something?'

'Mrs Trefusis,' Arthur decided. 'She owns the hotel. She's a grumpy old woman, but she'll help.'

'How do you know it wasn't her that just went for us?' Sarah wanted to know.

Arthur gave a short laugh. 'She's about ninety,' he said. 'And she's in a wheelchair. If we can be sure of anything, it's that Mrs Trefusis isn't running about killing people.'

They paused at the door to the hotel. 'You sure about this?' Sarah said.

'No,' Arthur admitted. 'Come on.'

Chapter 13

The handsome, elegant figure of Edward Sayers seemed far more threatening than the pathetic hunchback he had been moments earlier. Art and Meg had watched in horrified fascination as the crouched, distorted figure straightened. There was a sound like crunching bones and the gnarled hands seemed to open out. His mouth stretched into a cruel slash of a smile and he stepped towards them.

Art pulled Meg back. Sayers was blocking the only way out of the room, but perhaps they could get to the laboratory and barricade themselves inside. Art was just turning to leap over the bed and run for it when the door swung open again.

'Jonny!' Meg gasped with delight.

Flinch was with him, and also a young woman whom Art did not know. She was clutching a small handbag, pulling it open, reaching inside.

Sayers too had turned to look. He stared in open-mouthed amazement at the woman. 'Vera?'

'Hello, Edwin,' she said. She pulled a small

pistol from the handbag. 'How are you today?' she asked quietly.

'This is Miss Waters,' Jonny explained. He pushed past the woman, Flinch following him. 'She's been looking for her brother, Edwin Waters.'

'I think she's found him,' Art replied.

'Yes, thank goodness,' Jonny agreed.

'I thought he was called Sayers,' Flinch said, watching the pistol in the woman's hand. 'Is he Mr Waters really?'

'I've never been better,' Sayers was telling his sister.

'Good.' She lowered the pistol. 'I was afraid you might still be having second thoughts.'

He smiled and shook his head. 'Another dose and I think the effects will be permanent. No more doubts, no more angst.'

'I'm so pleased.' She lifted the pistol again. 'You should not have run away from me,' she said to her brother. 'You knew you had to take your medicine. It was all for the best. The very best.' But this time she was pointing the gun across the room – at Art and the others.

'What are you doing?' Jonny asked. He looked at Art, bemused and anxious.

'We'll need some more potion,' Miss Waters said, still holding the pistol levelled. 'And for that, we'll need blood of course.' She was smiling, mirroring her brother's expression. It was not pleasant. She turned to look at him, just for a moment.

But a moment was all that Art needed. 'Now!' he shouted. He pushed Meg and Flinch ahead of him across the bed and towards the back room. Jonny was close behind. A bullet cracked into the floor close behind him as Art flung himself into the laboratory. Seconds later, Meg slammed the door shut. Another crack, and a piece of wood splintered away and spun across the room.

In the corner, Old Toby was licking at the stained floor. He looked up at the children through rheumy eyes, then went back to his fruitless task.

Meg turned the key in the lock. Art and Jonny dragged over the nearest armchair from where it was pushed against the wall. They jammed it up against the door. Then Art jumped up on to it and put his ear to the door.

'There's no other way out,' Meg announced, looking round.

'There's the window,' Jonny said. He ran to open it. But like the one in the bedroom, it would only open a few inches. He would barely have been able to stick his head out and call for help. Anyway, the chances were no one would hear. And if they did, they would probably ignore him.

Art paid little attention. He was struggling to hear what was happening in the bedroom.

'What are they saying?' Flinch asked. 'Are they going to break the door down? Or shoot their way in? Hey, Art, why don't I try—'

He waved at her to be quiet. 'Flinch, please – I can't hear. Just be quiet, all of you. We need to know what they're up to.'

Flinch pulled a face and stomped off. Art sighed. He had upset her, but he wanted to hear what was going on.

'They're out for blood,' Meg said. 'Ours.'

'Why?' Jonny wanted to know.

'For their potion stuff.'

Art gave up. He could hear voices, but he could not make out the words.

'There's some potion here,' Jonny said. He was standing at the end of the table, close to where Old Toby was still washing the floor with his tongue. He pointed to the small glass beaker in which a dark red liquid dripped from the end of a tube. 'At least, I suppose that's what it is. His next batch, it must have been brewed or whatever while he was out.' Jonny's face brightened. 'Hey, why don't *we* drink it and get super powers or whatever happens?'

'Oh, good idea,' Meg told him sarcastically. 'Why don't we become addicted killers, doomed to roam the streets in search of blood?'

'It was just an idea,' Jonny protested.

'Yes,' Art said, 'well, we need all the ideas we can think of now. However daft they might seem. I really don't see a way out of this.' He sighed and forced a thin smile. 'Sorry I shouted at you just now.' His smile froze as he looked round the room. 'Where's Flinch gone?'

Apart from Meg, Jonny and Art, the room was empty. The only movement in the stunned silence was the edge of the curtain, blowing in the breeze from the barely open window.

It had been relatively easy for Flinch to squeeze herself out of the window. Since Art was busy and didn't want to listen to her idea, she decided to go ahead anyway.

As soon as she was perched on the windowledge, Flinch realised that there was no way she could climb down to the ground. There was a drainpipe running between this window and the next and she grabbed hold of it to stop herself losing her balance. But it was too far to try to climb down it. So instead she swung herself nimbly round it, to land her feet on the sill of the next window along – the window into the bedroom.

Crouching on the narrow ledge outside the window, Flinch could see into the room. Sayers and the woman, Miss Waters, were by the door into the back room, talking quietly. If Flinch could squeeze through the window without them noticing, she could make a run for the stairs outside.

But if they saw her . . . Even as Flinch considered this, Miss Waters raised the small pistol, jabbing it into the air as she made some point to her brother. Flinch swallowed.

It was harder to get back in than it had been to get out. The opening was just as wide, but Flinch had to manoeuvre herself while balancing on the thin ledge outside. She managed to get her arms and head through the window, wiggling her shoulders through after them. All the time she was conscious that Miss Waters had only to glance in her direction, Mr Sayers had only to look over from the door, and she would be trapped – half in and half out of the window.

But mercifully they seemed intent on trying to open the door. Sayers put his shoulder to it, but without effect. The muffled thud of his attempts to burst through the door masked the sound of Flinch falling through the window. She stayed below the height of the bed, holding her breath as she listened for any clue that she had been heard.

Eventually she risked a peep over the top of the bed. Sayers and his sister were still at the door. She was checking the gun – perhaps making sure it was fully loaded. As Flinch watched, the woman snapped the gun shut and turned back to the door. But, as she turned, she looked across – at the window. At where Flinch was looking out from behind the bed.

Immediately Flinch ducked down, but she knew she had been seen. She risked another quick glimpse – and saw Miss Waters walking slowly towards her, the gun raised.

Flinch screamed and ran.

At the same moment came the sound of breaking glass. A terrific crash from behind the locked door.

'They've broken the window,' Sayers said.

Miss Waters was turning. 'If it was the window.'

They were frozen by the thought and Flinch almost made it to the door. Almost.

'Get her!' Miss Waters screeched, and Sayers flung himself across the room to grab Flinch. His hand closed on her shoulder. She shrugged it off. But his other hand grabbed her wrist and pulled her back. Flinch struggled and yelled and thrashed and bit. But he held her tight, dragging her back towards the door.

His sister aimed the gun at the lock and fired. The wood exploded and the lock shattered.

Sayers threw Flinch into Miss Waters's arms and hurled himself at the door. The gun jabbed into Flinch's cheek. The door opened a fraction and he pushed again, knocking away the chair that was wedged behind it. The door crashed open.

Inside the room, Meg and Jonny were standing by the table. The delicate glassware was shattered and broken, pieces of broken glass strewn across the table and on the floor.

'No!' Sayers shouted. 'Stop!'

Miss Waters pushed Flinch away, towards the room, and brought the gun round to point into the back room. As she did so, Art stepped into the doorway. He was holding two glass flasks, his palms wrapped round them so it was impossible to tell what – if anything – they contained.

'Guess,' he said quietly. 'Left hand or right hand. Guess wrong and you'll have no more potion. Or,' he added, 'you can let us walk out of here and I'll let you have them both.'

But Miss Waters was in no mood to bargain. Flinch could see a nerve ticking by her eye as she answered. 'Never!' she spat, and the gun jerked in her hand as she fired.

Flinch screamed again. Art jumped to one side. The bullet just missed Art and thudded into the wall behind where Old Toby was still lapping at the floor. Meg and Jonny leaped aside. Art was moving now. He hurled one of the flasks towards Miss Waters as she aimed the gun again. The other he tossed, almost casually, over his shoulder.

The flask that Art had tossed away landed

close to Old Toby and shattered on the floor. A dark, sticky liquid spilled out and pooled on the wooden boards. The dog hobbled over and licked at it furiously, ignoring the shards of glass that bit into his tongue.

The other flask curled through the air towards Miss Waters. Desperate to catch it, she dropped the gun. Flinch could see the concentration on the woman's face as she cupped her hands to receive the spinning flask. Could see the expression turn to anger as she saw the liquid inside was not thick and red but clear like water. Watched the anger turn to horror as the liquid spilled from the spinning, unstoppered flask and splashed down on to her hand and forearm. Not water. Acid.

Miss Waters snatched her hand away and moved back as the flask landed. The floor started to smoke as the acid burned into the boards. She gave a screech of pain, her right hand and forearm also smoking as the acid burned a pattern. It scorched out the flesh of her forearm, tributaries of searing liquid running like roots into the smoking mess as the acid splashed and spat.

Flinch gasped as the woman collapsed to the

floor, clutching her arm. But before she could react further, before she could make a run for the door, Sayers had scooped up the fallen gun and was turning it towards Art and the others.

Meanwhile, Old Toby, his fur standing on end and the teeth he had lost years ago bared into a savage snarl, looked up from the pool of liquid on the floor. He saw Art, Jonny and Meg standing only feet away, and hurled himself forwards with a vicious bark of triumph – straight at Jonny.

They found Mrs Trefusis alone in the drawing room. She had her wheelchair positioned close to the fire and was staring into the flames, lost in her thoughts.

When Arthur and Sarah came in, she looked up and smiled. Arthur did not think he had seen her smile before, and he took this as a good omen. She did not seem surprised to see Sarah or to learn that she had come to visit Arthur. She listened quietly and attentively as Arthur, with help from Sarah, told her what sounded even to him like an increasingly improbable story of bungled kidnapping, attempted murder, arson, killing and assault.

'The telephones are still not working,' she said when Arthur had finished. 'Otherwise the obvious thing to do would be to call the police.'

'You believe us?' Sarah asked, incredulous.

Mrs Trefusis looked at her, eyes sharp and bright despite her age. 'I think there is too much detail and incident in what you say for me to dismiss it lightly.' She nodded thoughtfully. 'And I think you should shut and lock the door. After all, we have no idea whom we can trust.'

Arthur closed the door and locked it. The key was large and heavy but it turned easily in the lock. The door itself was thick, solid wood studded with metal. No one was going to get through that easily. Arthur realised that for the first time since he had arrived, he actually felt safe.

'Bring me the key, would you?' She placed it in her lap, turning the wheelchair so she could see Arthur and Sarah, who were now sitting on the faded leather sofa. The firelight threw patterns across the old lady's face, rippling like light on water. 'I wonder if we should close the shutters as well,' she suggested quietly. 'We can't be too careful.'

Together Arthur and Sarah swung the heavy panelled wooden shutters across. They unfolded from either side of the window, and at each window there was a heavy metal locking bar that came down across the shutters to hold them tight against the frame.

'What now?' Arthur wondered as they returned to the sofa. He was relieved that someone else had taken the initiative.

'Now we wait,' the old lady said. 'And while we have the time, we can perhaps work out what is happening and who we should be wary of.'

'Mr Huntingdon,' Arthur said. 'He gets my vote. He's been poking about all over the place since I arrived. He was up on the roof as well.'

'He does sound the most likely candidate,' Sarah agreed. She seemed to have relaxed as well, leaning back into the hard leather of the sofa.

Mrs Trefusis nodded. 'I agree his actions sound rather suspicious. But there may be some simple explanation.' She wheeled her chair over towards the low table where the tantalus containing the twin decanters stood together with a round silver tray on which six sherry glasses were arranged upside-down in a circle.

'Could you be ever so kind and pour me a glass of port?' Mrs Trefusis asked. 'All this excitement has made my throat quite dry. It may be a little early, but I think in the circumstances . . .'

'Of course.'

The tantalus was locked, but Mrs Trefusis pulled open a small drawer in the table to reveal a tiny key. Arthur unlocked the wooden front of the tantalus, which folded down so he could take out the decanters. One was empty, the other perhaps a third full. He turned over one of the glasses and poured a measure of the viscous red liquid.

Mrs Trefusis accepted the glass with a smile and sipped at her drink. 'That's better. Good. Thank you so very much.'

Arthur returned the smile. But it froze on his face and he felt his whole body suddenly shiver.

'You know,' the old woman was saying, 'Mr Huntingdon is actually from the South East branch of the Hoteliers and Vintners Association and is here to decide how many gold points we should get in the next edition of their guide. Though he thinks I don't know that. It is his job to go poking about, as you put it.'

But Arthur barely heard her words. He was

backing slowly away from her. As she accepted the glass, Arthur had noticed the old woman's forearm again. Noticed the pattern of scars – the scooped-out wrist with the skin stretched tight, the tributaries of dead tissue that ran like roots into the main scar ...

'You know, before I married,' the old lady went on, apparently oblivious to Arthur's disquiet, 'my maiden name was Waters. Vera Waters. Does that sound familiar?'

It did. It was a name Arthur had read – in the Invisible Detective's casebook, together with a description of how the acid had splashed and scarred. He felt suddenly cold as he remembered.

'What's going on?' Sarah asked anxiously as Arthur continued to back away.

'You only poured me a half-measure,' Mrs Trefusis accused. 'But no matter. I couldn't believe it when I saw you outside that school, Art Drake. Couldn't believe it was you. Even though I was working on the same problem, trying to preserve youth and health, I couldn't believe that you had not changed one bit.' She drained the last drop of red liquid from the glass and then hurled it aside.

'It's her!' Arthur shouted, grabbing Sarah's hand

and dragging her from the sofa. 'It was her all the time. She's completely mad!'

The glass shattered against the back of the fireplace, fragments falling into the burning logs. The flames flickered and danced as Mrs Trefusis rose from her wheelchair. She seemed younger, less frail, her knuckles clicking as she stretched her fingers and let out a sigh of satisfaction.

Sarah and Arthur were running, skidding round the furniture, slipping on a rug, almost knocking over a table. Running for the heavy wooden door. The door that Arthur had locked, he now remembered. And Mrs Trefusis had the key.

The old woman's voice was no longer the dry-leafed cackle it had been. Now it was strong and loud. 'Above all,' she said, as she started slowly across the room towards them, 'I could not believe that I would get a chance to avenge my brother. A chance to kill you.'

236

Chapter 14

With a shriek of anger and surprise, Jonny leaped to one side. Old Toby skidded to a halt, his claws clicking on the wooden floorboards. Jonny watched wide-eyed as the wild dog prepared to launch himself again.

Sayers seemed content to let Old Toby savage the boy. He was standing, watching, the gun in his hand. Beside him his sister was on her knees, clutching her forearm and gritting her teeth against the pain. Her whole body was shivering. But Sayers ignored her. Flinch was hesitating, not sure whether to run or try to help somehow. Meg seemed frozen in position.

So it was up to Art, he decided. He had only seconds to deal with Sayers, prevent Jonny from being mauled and find a way of escape. Acting on instinct rather than strategy, he grabbed the nearest thing and threw it as hard as he could at Sayers.

It was another flask – more clear liquid. He hoped it wasn't acid again. But whatever was in the flask, Sayers jumped out of the way, the gun no longer pointing at Art and the others. Old Toby caught sight of the flask as it spun through the air.

He paused in his pursuit of Jonny and watched it crash to the floor. Seeing the liquid spill out, he changed direction – Jonny forgotten – and hurled himself towards the door to the bedroom.

Thinking the dog was attacking him rather than racing for the liquid, Sayers quickly swung the gun. A shot cracked out, grazing the creature's back. But rather than slowing him, it angered him. Old Toby changed course once more – but only slightly – this time leaping at Sayers.

There was no time to fire before the dog's jaw clamped round Sayers's hand, dragging it and the gun downwards. Sayers gave a shout of pain, dropping the gun with a clatter.

'Come on!' Art pushed Meg towards the door and hauled Jonny to his feet. They ran, leaping over the prone figures of Sayers and his sister, who were now both wrestling with Old Toby. Sayers was battling to keep the dog from snapping at his throat, while Miss Waters was trying to drag the beast clear of her brother.

In a moment, Art and the others were past. Miss Waters made an effort to grab Meg's leg as she went by, but the girl kicked the woman away. Meg grabbed Flinch's hand and they all made a dash for the stairs. As she fell, Miss Waters scooped up the fallen gun and fired.

Art glanced back for just long enough to see Sayers finally manage to wrestle Old Toby's body off his own and struggle to his feet, the dog snapping again at the man's heels.

Then Art was following the others down the stairs. 'Jonny,' he shouted, 'go for help. Take Flinch.'

Jonny was already waiting at the bottom of the stairs. 'Where are you going?'

Behind them, they could all hear the thumping of feet on the stairs. 'Meg and I will try to lose them. But we'll lead them off anyway, to give you a chance to escape.'

'Make for the mirror maze,' Jonny called back. He was already racing for the end of the alley, pulling Flinch after him. 'Your dad might still be there.'

Meg had hoped they could lose themselves in the crowds at the fair, but it just wasn't possible. While Flinch and Jonny had faded quickly into the distance and out of sight, Sayers and Miss Waters were close on Meg's and Art's heels.

'Let's ask someone for help,' Meg gasped.

'Who'd believe us?' Art said. 'And we haven't time to explain.'

Sayers did not seem willing to use the gun in the crowds, but Meg was sure that, if they got within reach, he and Miss Waters would grab herself and Art, then drag them off to some spot where they could dispose of them with little fuss and no fear of being seen. They had, after all, nothing to lose.

Art led her a convoluted trail through the streets – round stalls and past sideshows. Even, at one point, across the coconut shy as people were hurling wooden balls. Meg ducked and ran, lucky not to be hit on the head. They raced past fire-eaters, leaped on the merry-go-round – to the annoyance of the man in charge – and went halfway round before jumping off again.

Eventually, Art slowed to a walk, breathing deeply. Meg struggled to catch her breath.

'I think we've lost them,' Art said.

'Thank goodness for that.'

They were just along the street from the performing apes. Judging by the assembled group and the applause that carried to them, the Mighty

240

Fred was going through his routine undeterred by his earlier unmasking.

'So what now?' Meg asked.

'Let's wait at the mirror maze for Jonny and Flinch,' Art decided. 'I doubt Dad's still there, but he might be, I suppose.'

'It's worth a look,' Meg agreed.

The police had gone. There was just the old lady huddled in her coat, sitting at the little table as before. She rattled the tin of coins without looking up as Art and Meg came in.

'I'll ask her if Jonny's been here yet,' Meg suggested.

Art nodded. After all, he might have been and gone again while they were chasing round outside. Meg would know if the woman was telling them the truth.

They went over to the table and Meg said politely, 'Excuse me—'

But she got no further.

The old lady stood up, her coat falling away to reveal the small pistol she was holding. 'Edwin told me you'd come here,' Miss Waters said, shrugging off the old woman's coat. 'Looking for Daddy?' she sneered.

241

Art seemed frozen to the spot, so Meg gave him an almighty shove in the back. He stumbled heavily through the door into the mirror maze, Meg running after. Miss Waters's laughter followed them.

They ducked behind a mirror, weaving their way deep into the maze.

'We know that no one can hide in here for very long,' Art whispered. 'There's no other way out.'

'We just need to keep out of sight.'

But Art was shaking his head. 'She said that Sayers knew we would come here.'

'So?'

'So I think he's here already. In the maze.' Art was looking round, studying the myriad reflections of himself and Meg. 'Waiting for us.'

Watching the old woman coming across the room towards him, Arthur could believe she had been the whirlwind disguised in coat and hat that had knocked Bill unconscious. Sarah ran one way, Arthur the other, forcing Mrs Trefusis to choose between them.

She did not hesitate. She went for Arthur.

'My biggest problem, once I had sent your father off on his wild goose chase, was getting away from Miss Napier,' the old woman said as she stalked after Arthur. 'I could get away at night, when she was asleep. And when I saw you alone in the library I managed to give her the slip. But I couldn't let her know what I was planning.'

'And what was that?' Arthur asked, dodging quickly round an armchair.

'Why, to kill you, of course.' She laughed – a dry, rasping cackle. 'It's very good of you to make it so easy after all this time. I have, I confess, savoured the anticipation.'

Sarah was tugging and pulling and hammering at the door, but to no avail.

Across the room, Arthur was still backing away from the old woman. 'The decanter,' he shouted. 'She said it was only a small measure.'

Mrs Trefusis was so intent on Arthur that she did not seem to realise what he meant. But Sarah did. She ran to the low table where the tantalus was still unlocked and pulled out the decanter of port.

Except of course it wasn't port. Mrs Trefusis had seen her now and was reluctantly leaving Arthur to rush across at Sarah, arms out to grab the decanter.

But before she got there, Sarah let the decanter drop. It hit the wooden floor, bounced, fell again. Shattered. The thick liquid splashed and ran across the floor, and Mrs Trefusis gave a cry of rage.

Sarah was already with Arthur on the other side of the sofa. They kept it between them and Mrs Trefusis as she circled and glared and waited for an opportunity to grab them.

As they circled, keeping close to the large leather sofa, Arthur caught sight of something out of the corner of his eye. Something that lay on the floor in front of the abandoned wheelchair. Something that had dropped from her lap when Mrs Trefusis stood up. He nudged Sarah, not wanting to point but hoping she could see it too.

'How long will a short measure last?' Sarah whispered.

Had she seen?

'Long enough,' Mrs Trefusis spat back at her. As she spoke she leaped across the sofa, her agility belying her apparently old and frail form.

Again, Sarah and Arthur scattered. Sarah ran back towards the door. Arthur went for the key. It was lying where it had fallen when the old woman stood up. He snatched it from the floor, ducked under Mrs Trefusis's arm as it lashed out at him and threw the key across the room to Sarah.

She caught it, then almost dropped it, but she managed to hold on. She jammed it into the lock and struggled to turn it.

Arthur dashed across the room, with Mrs Trefusis close behind him. Sarah had the door open just in time for Arthur to dive through. She followed, slamming the door behind them.

Except that it did not shut. Mrs Trefusis had her shoulder to it and was pushing it open again with incredible strength. Arthur and Sarah both heaved against the door, but it was slowly and inexorably inching open. Arthur looked round for something to jam against the door, to halt its progress. But there was nothing.

'What's going on?' Mr Huntingdon was coming along the hallway. 'Have you got someone trapped in there?' he demanded.

'I wish,' Arthur gasped. Another inch or two open . . .

'Help us, please,' Sarah pleaded. 'If she gets out, she'll kill us!'

Mr Huntingdon stared at them as if they were mad. Then he took hold of Arthur by the shoulders and heaved him out of the way.

'No!' Arthur shouted, as he stumbled and fell.

Realising that she could not hold the door any longer without Arthur to help, Sarah leaped aside. The door crashed open, catching Mr Huntingdon on the chin and sending him reeling backwards with a cry of pain. He crashed into the opposite wall and slumped motionless to the ground.

'That saves some explanations,' Arthur mumbled. He was back on his feet, grabbing Sarah by the hand. They ran together down the hall and out of the front door – into the snow.

Behind them, Mrs Trefusis spared the unconscious Mr Huntingdon no more than a passing glance before running after them.

They headed for the trees. The snow crunched under their desperate feet.

'Maybe we can hide,' Arthur said.

'Don't be stupid,' Sarah told him. 'She'll follow our tracks in the snow.'

'Maybe we can get to the shed. Find something to defend ourselves with.'

Sarah grunted a response. It might have been agreement or more derision. But she ran with Arthur into the wood and back towards the shed.

Except it wasn't there.

'Must be further in,' Arthur said. 'We came into the wood at a different angle.'

'Follow the tracks,' Sarah told him. 'That's where we followed her back to the house.' She pointed to the scuffed trail that crossed in front of them. 'It must be that way. Come on.'

They had wasted precious seconds, but there seemed to be no sign that Mrs Trefusis was coming after them. Perhaps she was tiring, the effects of the potion wearing off. Perhaps . . .

The real reason, Arthur realised, as soon as the shed came into sight, was that she had known where they were making for and how to get there quickly. As they broke through the ring of trees, the old woman stepped out from behind the shed. Her face was set in a grimace that seemed to combine both anger and satisfaction.

There was no time to stop. Running as fast as they were, Arthur and Sarah were unable to change direction. They skidded as their feet slid from under them. Mrs Trefusis spread her arms wide, as if to gather them in. Arthur felt her grab his arm and drag him towards her.

Then he was falling, crashing to the ground in a tangled mass, rolling and sliding with Sarah and Mrs Trefusis. The old woman's breath was unpleasantly warm on his face as she clamped him to her, her sharp nails biting into his neck as she clutched at his throat.

With an almighty effort, Arthur tore himself free. He heaved at Sarah's arm, pulling her up and away from the woman's claws.

As soon as Sarah was free, Arthur turned to run. But Sarah did not move. Instead she pulled him back and said, 'Look.'

Arthur looked.

Mrs Trefusis was snarling with rage, her jaw snapping like an angry dog's. She was pushing at the ground, frantically thrashing and rolling. But her legs were still.

'She can't get up,' Arthur realised. 'The effect must be wearing off.'

'Help me!' The old woman's voice was cracked and brittle like autumn leaves. 'Help an old lady.'

'You must be joking,' Sarah said.

'We'll get someone,' Arthur promised. He backed away, unwilling to take his eyes off her in case this was a ruse, in case as soon as he turned she leaped up and chased after him – her hands ready to close again on his throat . . .

The wheelchair left tracks in the snow like railway lines. Miss Napier had it tipped back on its large rear wheels and navigated with practised ease through the snow. They had found her locked in her room and she had seemed genuinely relieved to see Arthur.

'I found her outside your room last night,' Miss Napier confessed. 'That's why I asked if you were all right, after I'd put her back to bed. I realised, of course, she must be distilling the potion again.'

They collected the wheelchair from the drawing room, pausing while Miss Napier inspected Mr Huntingdon's bruised chin and the cut on the back of his head. She sent Arthur to sort out a cold, wet flannel.

'She hadn't touched the stuff in years,' Miss Napier said sadly as they made their way across the white lawn towards the wood. 'She met Dr Trefusis during the Second World War. He treated her for mental illness, but he soon realised she wasn't really ill. Just bitter. He fell in love with her and got her released. They were happy for many years. But as she grew older, so she thought more and more about what the potion could do for her. When her husband died, she started again.'

They continued in silence for a while. In the distance, on the other side of the lawn, Arthur could see a car making its ponderous way along the snowy drive.

'I managed to wean her off it,' Miss Napier said sadly. 'I thought it was all over, all in the past.'

'But then she saw Arthur,' Sarah said. 'And assumed he was Art. Still young.'

'She thought Arthur had perfected a form of the potion that had kept him young. She was livid. So angry. At least, that was what I thought. But in fact, of course, it drove her completely mad.'

'Again,' Arthur muttered.

'Bill wanted to warn you,' Miss Napier went on. 'Then he wanted to leave. But I persuaded him it would be better if he stayed and helped.'

The car was level with them now, the drive swinging round towards the front of the hotel. It was a car he recognised.

'Dad!'

'You go,' Miss Napier said. 'I can manage.'

'What about Mr Ashe?' Arthur said.

'And Bill and Mr Huntingdon?'

'The murder will need explaining,' Miss Napier conceded.

Dad was out of the car now, waving at Arthur. He waved back.

'She can't be allowed to get away with it.'

'I agree,' Sarah said. 'She tried to kill us too.'

Miss Napier nodded sadly. 'You are right, of course. But you had better go. I will sort everything out. Properly. Trust me.'

'For good,' Arthur insisted.

Miss Napier pushed the wheelchair forwards. 'Yes,' she said quietly. 'For good. I think it is for the best.' She paused and turned to Arthur. 'You go. There is a path to the shed from the other side. I shall be fine now. I can manage.'

Dad did not want to linger. He and Arthur collected their things while Arthur and Sarah gave a garbled and probably not very convincing explanation for Sarah's presence.

Mr Huntingdon was sitting in the drawing room. He was pressing a wet handkerchief to his head with his left hand while with his right he scribbled furiously on a small notepad. Arthur went to say goodbye, but the man spared him little more than a glance. He was muttering under his breath as he wrote and Arthur caught odd words and phrases: '. . . anything like it . . . health and safety . . . fire, food poisoning, phones . . .'

'Well, bye, then,' Arthur said when it became obvious that Mr Huntingdon was not going to acknowledge him.

Mr Peters was fussing round in the hallway, rubbing his hands and insisting that everything was fine. But despite his assurances, the Smiths were demanding their bill.

'The roads are obviously clear if he can get back again,' Mr Smith said, pointing at Arthur's dad. He frowned at Sarah, who smiled back at him politely.

Mrs Smith made a comment about the weekend not having been what she had expected. Then she left the two men to it and went out, leaving the suitcases for Mr Smith, who was insisting on paying in cash.

'I assume there's no bill to pay,' Arthur's dad told Mr Peters. He did not wait for an answer, but led Arthur and Sarah out to the car.

Arthur waved to Mrs Smith, who was waiting impatiently outside the door. She did not wave back.

They drove away in silence. The snow was beginning to fall again and through the tumbling white flakes Arthur caught sight of the shed. He wasn't certain, but he fancied he could see the wheelchair parked outside it. He thought he could make out Miss Napier, standing beside the empty chair, looking down at a huddled figure lying motionless in the snow. He fancied she was crying and could imagine the cold tears freezing on her cheeks.

'It's supposed to get warmer tomorrow,' Dad said as they turned out of the drive and on to the main road.

Chapter 15

Dozens of guns were pointing at Art and Meg. Reflections of reflections of reflections.

'Come on!' Art hissed, and the two of them ran further into the maze. Art drew up just short of running into himself – a mirror image that reflected his worried features.

'You're right,' Meg said. 'They'll find us sooner or later.'

'Let's hope it's later.'

'She isn't following us.'

'No,' Art agreed. 'She's staying near the entrance, so we can't slip out while the two of them are hunting for us in here.'

'Where's Sayers, do you suppose?' Meg was looking round – Art could see the turn of her head and the swing of her hair several times over.

'Right here.' The voice made them both jump.

Behind one of the reflections of Meg, Art could see the shadowy form of Sayers as he stalked towards them.

'You can't get away,' the voice said.

Art tried to remember which side the man's

hair was parted. Was it him or a reflection? Or was it a reflection of a reflection, in which case it made no difference? But if they ran away from him, they might paradoxically be running straight to him. Like Alice always ending up at the front door when she walked away from the house in Looking-Glass Land.

Meg was obviously having similar thoughts. 'You can't tell the real from the reflection,' she said.

There was the glimmer of an idea forming at the back of Art's mind. 'No,' he said. 'No, you can't.'

Jonny was running, slowing occasionally for Flinch to catch him up, then dashing off again. They ran through the crowds at the fair, looking round all the time for a policeman.

'There's usually loads of them,' Flinch insisted.

'But not today.' Jonny paused, turning a full circle as he looked.

'There – look,' Flinch gasped. 'It's Charlie.'

He was standing with his back to them, watching a Punch and Judy show. Flinch had seen it before. It was quite good, except when Mr Punch hit Judy. Meg had almost cried at that bit – reminded, Flinch guessed, of her life at home. Charlie's distinctive mass of white hair was visible above the small crowd of onlookers.

'Thank goodness,' Jonny said.

Together they ran over and Jonny called Charlie's name. They pushed through the people and Jonny grabbed the man's arm, pulling him round, shaking him urgently, shouting.

But it wasn't Charlie at all. The man was a complete stranger.

Meg had no idea what Art was up to. He had led her back the way they had come, towards the entrance to the mirror maze – towards where Miss Waters was waiting for them with the gun. The reflection of Sayers had stepped out of view, perhaps following a reflection of Art and Meg. Or perhaps he was even now closing on them.

Art was frowning, taking quick looks behind mirrors as they negotiated the maze.

'What are you looking for?'

'I need to know where the real Sayers is,' he told her. 'I just hope he's seen us.'

'What?'

He waved her to silence. 'Nearly there,' he whispered. 'Meg, I think you'd better wait here.' He took her by the shoulders and steered her into a corner.

'Why? What are you going to do?'

'I hope I can lure Miss Waters into the maze. If I do, then you can slip out behind her when she comes after me.'

'She'll probably shoot you!' Meg told him.

But Art was gone, slipped behind a mirror, and not even a reflection remained. Just his voice, floating back through the maze: 'I'm counting on it.'

Meg waited for almost a minute, then anxiety got the better of her and she walked slowly in the direction Art had taken. They were indeed near the entrance now. She could see reflections of Miss Waters standing with the gun out in front of her. She seemed to be aiming at something.

Meg ducked back out of sight, she hoped. It was impossible to tell who could see what among the forest of mirrors. As she moved, she caught sight of Art. He was standing not ten feet away, looking in the other direction. He had not seen Meg.

Nor had he seen Miss Waters. Moving forwards slightly, Meg could see that it was Art she was aiming at. The gun levelled. Her hands tight round it. Finger tightening on the trigger as she smiled with unpleasant satisfaction.

'Art!' Meg screamed.

Art whirled round, seemed to catch sight of Miss Waters and the gun. Froze.

She fired, twice. Straight at Art. So close there was no way she could miss.

Only it wasn't Art at all. It was his reflection.

The mirror exploded under the impact of the first bullet. Shards of glass blizzarded down and Meg threw herself to the floor. She covered her face with her hands, felt the sting of slivers of glass on her skin. Between her fingers she saw the air clear as the glass fell to reveal Sayers standing behind the mirror, reaching out for Art – the real Art.

The look of malevolent satisfaction on the man's face as he lunged towards Art turned into shock and surprise as the second bullet caught him in the chest. It knocked him sideways, crashing into another mirror, falling to the floor.

The gun clattered as Miss Waters dropped it.

She screamed, was running, crouching in the broken glass beside her dying brother, cradling his head in her hands as his eyes glazed over and her tears dripped on to his cold cheeks.

'Are you all right, Meg?'

She turned to see Art was now standing beside her. 'You beast!' she hissed angrily. 'Never do anything like that again.' Then she laughed at his bemused expression, almost crying with relief.

She was wiping the tears from her eyes when, moments later, Jonny and Flinch came running in. Art's dad and several policemen were close behind them.

'Jonny nearly got arrested for annoying an old man,' Flinch said, and Meg laughed again.

'She's a resourceful young lady,' Grandad remarked. 'Reminds me of Meg, actually.'

Sarah was sitting cross-legged on the bed in Arthur's grandad's small room at the home. She tilted her head to one side, her long black hair falling away.

'Lucky for you,' Sarah said. 'Otherwise you might still be locked in your room, afraid to go down for breakfast.'

Arthur did not reply to this. 'I suppose,' he said instead, 'that Mrs Trefusis – Miss Waters as she was then – was locked up in some mental institution.'

'Yes,' Grandad said. He looked round. 'Probably somewhere a bit like this.'

'Oh, I don't think so,' Arthur said quickly.

'He's joking,' Sarah explained, and Arthur was embarrassed to see that Grandad was smiling in agreement. 'I suppose,' she went on, 'that she was really after the elixir of life. Sorting out her brother was one thing, but she wanted to live for ever.'

'Living for ever may not be that good a deal,' Grandad replied. 'It's eternal youth that's important.'

'She thought I'd managed it,' Arthur said. 'Mistook me for you.'

'It's a trade-off,' Grandad decided. 'Experience for age. You don't get one without the other. A fact of life. And death,' he added with a sigh.

'You've got years yet,' Sarah assured him.

'You never can tell,' Grandad said. 'That's the thing. Mind you,' he went on, 'if it's eternal life she was after, she'd have done better to use the Book of Anubis.'

'The what?' Arthur asked. He had never heard of the Book of Anubis. Or had he? Somehow it sounded familiar. Like something he might once have read about or dreamed of.

Grandad was smiling. He looked at Arthur and then at Sarah. 'Well,' he said, 'perhaps that is a story for another day.'

Flinch sat cross-legged on the floor in the gap between the curtains and the bay window, trying not to smile as Jonny and Meg hissed and whispered at each other. Meg was complaining that Jonny looked as if he was about to drop the fishing rod. Jonny was telling Meg that she worried too much. Meg was annoyed that he kept talking and Jonny was cross that Meg seemed to ignore what he said.

On the other side of the curtain, Albert Norris recounted the sad tale of the discovery of Elsie's body in Mr Sayers's rooms above the pub. The

Invisible Detective took up the story and explained that Mr Sayers had been responsible, though he was ill.

'Mental,' someone muttered close to the curtain.

'Should have been on medicine,' someone else said.

But Flinch knew it had been the medicine that was making him ill. Without it, he might have been crippled and awkward but he would have been *well*.

Then Brandon Lake talked briefly about the Hunchback of Cricklewood. He explained that the hunchback would not be causing any more trouble and that a young woman was also helping the police with their enquiries. He could say nothing else.

But Art had told the Cannoniers more than that. His father had said that Miss Waters claimed she knew about the potion from an old book and had tested it on her misshapen brother. She had hoped to be able to stay young for ever and to cure what she saw as her brother's illness. But instead she had driven him – and herself – mad.

'I'd like to know,' Albert Norris was asking, 'whether all this has got anything to do with Old Toby being so out of sorts recently. He seems back to normal now, though he's taken to moping about in that awful man's old room above the pub.'

Meg and Jonny had stopped bickering and were listening with rapt attention now as the Invisible Detective assured his audience that Old Toby would be fine. Apart from the graze down his back. This drew a startled gasp from Norris, who proclaimed loudly that Old Toby did have a graze on his back but how could the detective possibly know that?

'How indeed?' Jonny whispered to Meg.

Flinch joined them close to the curtain. She smiled up at Jonny and he grinned back at her. Meg's face was set in a mild frown, which seemed to be its natural state. But when she saw Flinch beside her, she too smiled. Flinch grinned back at each of them, and she stared at the curtain so hard she thought she might be able to see through it – to see the Invisible Detective himself, in his armchair with its back to the audience as he enthralled and thrilled them with his stories of mystery and mischief in London.

Yes, Flinch thought, it was good that the people had the Invisible Detective to help them and listen to their problems. And it was good that she had Art and Meg and Jonny – the three best friends anyone could ask for – here with her in a dimly lit room above a locksmith's shop on Cannon Street on a cold Monday evening early in 1937.